the house on the gulf

the
house
on the
gulf

MARGARET PETERSON HADDIX

SCHOLASTIC INC.

New York   Toronto   London   Auckland   Sydney
Mexico City   New Delhi   Hong Kong   Buenos Aires

For the Bonifanti family, who loaned a house and gave me an idea

With thanks to Kara Winton, Karen Ryan, and Scarlett LaCava for their help in researching this book

Bran was up to something.

I knew it the first day he showed me the house. He was speeding ahead of me on his bike, while I struggled and sweated behind him, huffing and puffing because even after three months in Florida I still wasn't used to the heat. I didn't know how Bran could be either, but my brother seemed to do everything right, even if it meant not sweating in 90-degree heat, with 90-percent humidity. Then suddenly he slammed on his brakes.

"Wait—," he said, placing both feet firmly on the sidewalk.

My bike's an old one we got at a yard sale, and the brakes are a little iffy, so I practically ran into him as I screeched to a halt.

"What do you mean, 'Wait'?" I asked. "Is this it?"

I looked at the house beside us, a flat-roofed, concrete-block cube painted lime green. We'd lived worse places. Heck, we were living in a worse place now.

"No," Bran said. "It's a lot nicer than that. Up there. The yellow one." He inclined his head ever so slightly. I guessed he meant a sunshine-colored house in the next block, mostly hidden by palm trees. Trust Bran to be the only sixteen-year-old on the planet to still remember—and obey—those grade school lectures about it being rude to point.

"Call me crazy," I said, "but wouldn't it be a lot easier to see the place if we were, say, in front of it?"

My brother fixed me with a patient-Bran look. He's been giving me those looks, I think, since I was a baby and he was four and I would take his toys. Mom swears he never hit me, never grabbed them back; just looked disappointed and patiently tried to explain to me why I'd done something wrong. From anyone else, those looks would be maddening. But it's hard to get very mad at Bran.

Even when I was a baby, Mom says, he almost always talked me into giving his toys back.

Now he shook his head.

"Not yet. I have to make sure . . . ," he said. He leaned forward, peering toward the house. I didn't have the slightest clue what he was making sure *of*, but after a few minutes he relaxed a little and said, "Okay, let's go."

We inched our bikes forward and crossed the street. The house looked better and better the closer we got to it. The yellow stucco seemed to gleam in the sunlight, and the palm fronds swayed gently against the windowpanes.

"Wow." I breathed. "I can't believe the Marquises are going to let us live here for free, all summer long."

Bran looked around like he was afraid someone would overhear me bragging and take away our great deal. But the street was deserted—all the people who were used to living in Florida knew enough to stay out of the heat.

"For free?" he asked. "They're *paying* us, remember?"

There was a little edge to his voice. He was so proud of the arrangement he'd worked out, the miracle he'd wrought. House-sitting, it was called. The whole concept was new to me. I'd never heard of someone letting you live somewhere without expecting you to pay for it. But the Marquises were a retired couple who lived in Florida in the winter and New York in the summer, and they'd gotten worried about a rash of burglaries on empty houses. So they were paying Bran to stay here and take care of the house while they were away. And they were letting Mom and me live here, too. It was about the most wonderful thing that had ever happened to our family.

I remember the night Bran announced he'd gotten this house-sitting job. Mom and I just stared at him for maybe five minutes straight. We were eating dinner, and we practically stopped with the forkfuls of Hamburger Helper halfway to our mouths. But Bran kept talking about what he'd figured out, revealing each detail like a magician pulling rabbits out of a hat.

"Mom, if we don't have to pay any rent, and if I'm working at the restaurant, you can go to school full-time this summer. And then—"

"I could qualify for the scholarship this year," Mom said slowly, as if in a trance. The scholarship was just about all Mom had talked about since we'd moved to Florida. She'd been trying to finish college for longer than I've been alive, but there'd never been enough money for that. When she heard about the school down here offering a special scholarship for single mothers, she nearly flipped out. She said that they must have written the guidelines just for her—except that she had to be a junior, and after thirteen years of trying, she only had enough credits to be a sophomore.

"See, Mom, it could all work out perfectly," Bran had finished excitedly.

But Mom shook her head. The trance was over.

"I can't let you do that," she'd said. "You're only sixteen. It's not fair to make you support your whole family. Not when I can be working, too."

"You wouldn't be making me," Bran said quietly. "I want to do this."

He sounded so dignified and noble that I felt a surge of pride. Bran would do anything to help Mom or me. I was really lucky to have a brother like that.

But Mom was still shaking her head.

"You need to save your money for your own college fund."

"But, Mom—" Any other kid would have sounded whiny saying that. Not Bran. He sounded downright authoritative. "You've got to look at the big picture. You said yourself that that scholarship will pay more in living expenses than you can make as a waitress. So the sooner you get the scholarship, the more money we'll have as a family. And you know I'll find a way to pay for college."

Mom could have seen that as an insult—Bran would find a way to pay for college, even if she hadn't. I've seen other mothers who would have flown off the handle at that: "Oh yeah? You think you're better than me? Just forget the whole thing!" Back in Pennsylvania, my friend Wendy's mother was the worst one in their whole house about slamming doors and stomping up the stairs. But my mom's not like that. She just tilted her head and gave Bran a sad little smile and said, "Okay. I won't rule out anything yet. Let's figure this out rationally." She pushed the dinner dishes aside, and they got out a pencil and paper and started calculating how much Bran could make in tips, what we'd save in rent, how much it'd cost to move again in the fall. I watched the numbers lining up on the paper, and even I could tell what was going to happen. The excitement in their voices was contagious. I grabbed Mom's hands and started dancing around the room with her, singing, "Mom's getting the scholarship! Mom's getting the scholarship!"

Laughing, Mom dropped my hands and declared, "Goodness. I wish everyone had as much confidence in me as you two do."

Mom says things like that—*goodness, good grief,* even *my gracious*—that make her sound about two billion years old. But she's only thirty-three, and looks probably ten years younger. She's got wavy blond hair and greenish eyes that almost glow when she's excited. Back in Pennsylvania the college boys were always hitting on her. I once heard Mom's friend Carlene say, "Honey, if I looked like you I'd be a model, not a mommy." Mom had just laughed. What she really wants to be is a doctor.

All that was running through my mind as Bran and I rolled our bikes toward the house.

"I'll show you the backyard first," Bran said.

We leaned our bikes against the side of the house and followed first the narrow driveway, then a short sidewalk that led around the corner. A small square of neatly mowed grass lay between a screened-in sunporch, a small shed, the driveway, and a chain-link fence that separated the Marquises' yard from their neighbors'.

"So this is where it all started, huh?" I kidded Bran. He'd gotten to know the Marquises in the first place because he'd offered to mow their lawn.

"Yes, I—," Bran started, then broke off as he whirled around to face the house. Someone was inside, rattling the doorknob of the back door. And then that someone stepped outside.

It was an old man. Later I'd wish that I'd looked at him more closely, that I'd studied his face carefully, memorized every detail. But at that moment, all I really noticed was that he was old.

"M-Mr. Marquis," Bran stammered. Bran never stammers. He almost choked on the last syllable of Mr. Marquis's name. "You scared me. I didn't see your car. I didn't know anyone was home. I thought you were leaving for New York yesterday. I—I thought you were a burglar or something."

He didn't seem relieved that it was Mr. Marquis instead of a burglar. He kept looking back and forth between me and Mr. Marquis.

Mr. Marquis chuckled.

"You are conscientious, aren't you?" he asked. "I don't think the yard's grown much since you mowed on Thursday. Remember, overmowing can be as bad for a yard as ignoring it. So just follow the schedule I gave you. No more, no less. All right?"

"Yes, sir," Bran said. "I wasn't planning to mow today. I was just, uh, checking up on the yard. I know it's a constant battle to keep it alive in this salt air. Just like you told me."

Something was wrong. Usually Bran was great with grownups—not just polite and respectful, like you're supposed to be, but actually comfortable talking to them. But now he was so shaken he hadn't even remembered to introduce me.

That bothered me. I wanted Mr. Marquis to know that I'd be conscientious living here too, that all of us intended to take good care of his property. I wanted him to know how much living here was going to mean to us.

"Excuse me," I said carefully. Unlike Bran, I am not usually all that comfortable talking to grown-ups. "I'm Bran's sister, Britt—well, Brittany, really—and—"

"Oh, yes, this is my sister," Bran interrupted. "Sorry. Sis, could you go take our bikes back out to the front sidewalk and wait there? I just need to talk to Mr. Marquis about a few details. We'll be quick, I promise."

My face flamed red, suddenly as hot as the Florida sun. Here I was trying to be so polite and mature, and Bran had interrupted me. *He'd* been rude! And why? It was almost like he didn't trust me to talk to Mr. Marquis, didn't trust me to hear the details of his house-sitting job. What could be so secret? Shouldn't I know everything, since I was going to be living in the house too?

And when had Bran ever called me *sis* before?

It was on the tip of my tongue to tell Bran off, to totally let him have it. But then I saw Mr. Marquis looking at us. He had big bushy gray eyebrows—I did notice those, at least—and they were squinted together like he was puzzled.

What if he went from being puzzled to being angry, and then decided we couldn't live in his house for the summer after all?

"Okay," I said meekly, though it felt like my innards were boiling.

I obediently walked around the corner of the house, but I didn't move the bikes right away. I stood still, just out of Bran's sight, and listened.

"Sorry," Bran was apologizing again. "We didn't mean to bother you. We'll be leaving in just a minute. Didn't you feel well enough to travel yesterday?"

That sounded more like the Bran I knew, polite and considerate.

Mr. Marquis's reply was a dim rumble—something about a

freak spring snowstorm in Tennessee—and then, a little louder, "But the Weather Channel says the ice has melted now, so we're leaving as soon as Mary gets back from the beauty parlor. Women! She already had her hair appointment made up North and was fretting so over having to cancel it. I told her to go ahead down here; we could wait another hour. . . ."

Why didn't Bran want me to hear that?

I got scared that any minute now, Bran would come around the corner and catch me eavesdropping, so I wheeled his bike out to the sidewalk. When I was coming back for my bike, I heard Mr. Marquis saying, "And don't lose the key—"

Wouldn't he want to make sure that Mom and I didn't lose our keys either?

"I won't, sir," Bran said. "Good-bye. Have a safe trip."

I ran my bike out toward the curb. A second later, Bran rounded the corner of the house and came up behind me.

"What was that all about?" I asked.

"Nothing," Bran muttered. "Come on. We need to get home now."

"But I haven't seen inside the house! Why'd we ride all the way over here if—"

"Ssh," Bran said. Rude again. He still looked spooked, too. "We don't want to intrude. I didn't know they hadn't left yet. They're probably still packing."

"But wouldn't they be done packing if they were planning to leave yesterday?"

It wasn't like me to persist. But I was still steamed about being banished to the sidewalk.

"Brittany," Bran said, and his voice was like steel. "I said, come on."

I swung my right leg over my bike seat, but I didn't start pedaling. I sat there, balanced on my bike seat, trying to decide what to do. I still think about what might have happened if I'd ignored Bran, strutted up to the Marquises' front door, begged to be let in.

But I was used to doing what Bran told me. And something about the house had already been ruined for me because of the way Bran was acting. I really didn't want to see inside it that day, with Mr. Marquis watching us.

"Okay," I relented, and pushed off, launching my bike into the empty street.

Bran zoomed ahead of me, leading the way, as always. And only then did I notice: He was sweating now. Pedaling out to the house in 90-degree heat hadn't made him lose his cool, but standing there talking to Mr. Marquis had given him rings of sweat on his T-shirt, rivers of sweat down the back of his neck. I'd never seen him sweat so much in my entire life.

Later I would wonder which had made him sweat more— talking to Mr. Marquis or being scared of Mr. Marquis talking to me?

2

That night Mom and I started packing
while Bran was at work. In the three months since we'd come
to Florida, we hadn't unpacked much to begin with—though
none of us said it out loud, we all knew that if you live in a
place like Sunset Terrace, you want to hold on to the notion
that you might be taking off for someplace better any minute.
There was mold on the walls we hadn't been able to get off with
any amount of scrubbing. Someone had punched a hole in the
bedroom door. The air-conditioning had a sickly wheeze and
rattle that made it sound like each breath of lukewarm air it
blew at us might be the last. And the walls were so thin we
could hear the neighbors fighting all night long. But apartments cost a lot more in Gulfstone than Mom had expected, so
we'd been making do. As Mom said about our move to Florida,
"Once again, the planning wasn't perfect."

But I could tell by the little grin that kept bursting onto
Mom's face that she thought the plans for the summer were as
close to perfect as possible. She folded clothes twice as fast as I
did and stacked them in the grocery store boxes with amazing
energy, especially considering she'd been at work ten hours
that day and had used her lunch break to sign up for all her
summer classes. She hummed while she worked.

I didn't want to worry her, didn't want to ruin her mood.

But I couldn't get Bran's odd behavior out of my mind.

"Bran showed me the house today," I said, starting out cautiously. "Just the outside, because Mr. Marquis was still there."

Would Mom think that sounded suspicious? Was that enough to start up the same alarm bells in her mind that were going off in mine?

Probably not.

"Um-hm," she said vaguely. "Nice, isn't it?"

"You haven't seen inside either, have you?" I asked.

"No," she said. "Bran drove me there back in March, I think, when he first started working for the Marquises. We rang the doorbell, but the Marquises weren't home. I don't know where you were then—volleyball practice, maybe?"

I'd joined the volleyball team at my new school in a desperate attempt to make friends. It hadn't worked, and I'd hated volleyball—hated the ball smacking my arms, hated the other girls screaming out, "It's mine, it's mine!" around me, because they'd already figured out that I wasn't any good.

Bran, meanwhile, had made tons of friends at the high school. The Computer Club had welcomed him with open arms; the Drama Club had been delighted at his expertise with the sound system for their plays.

I tried not to think about school.

"Don't you think it's a little . . . strange that you've never even met the Marquises, and we're going to be living in their house?" I was inching closer to something I hadn't quite let myself think yet.

"Well, kind of," Mom conceded. "But between my work schedule and their—what did Bran call it?—their 'social calendar,' it never worked out. I guess they're the kind of people who

11

are always going to their canasta club and their backgammon tournaments and all that." She grinned, stopping just short of making fun of the Marquises. I'd learned from the kids at school that there was a whole stereotype about old people down here. Supposedly they all went to dinner at four o'clock, and drove five miles per hour even when the speed limit was fifty-five, and, yes, spent most of their time playing canasta and backgammon and games like that.

"But you talked to Mr. Marquis on the phone, right?" I persisted.

"Sure," Mom said. "I wouldn't have felt right about this house-sitting deal at all if I hadn't at least done that."

I realized that I'd just been standing there holding the shirt I was supposed to be folding. I flipped it over, tucked it into the box, and dropped the hanger onto the stack on the floor. But I didn't pick up a new shirt to fold just yet.

"What did you think of Mr. Marquis?" I asked.

Mom shrugged.

"He seemed nice enough. A little hard of hearing, maybe. Kept shouting out, 'What's that?' and 'Eh?' when I was telling him we'd do our best to take care of his house, and how much the job meant to us. Honestly, it was all I could do not to laugh, so I probably didn't talk to him as long as I would have otherwise." Mom grinned again. "But there wasn't that much I needed to discuss with him, because Bran'll be the one doing all the work."

I couldn't quite bring myself to grin back at Mom. Mr. Marquis hadn't seemed the least bit hard of hearing when I'd met him. But maybe it's easier to hide deafness when you're talking to someone face-to-face, instead of over the phone.

"Kitchen now?" Mom said.

"What? Oh, okay," I said. We were done folding clothes, and I hadn't even noticed. I followed Mom toward the tiny cubbyhole that passed for a kitchen in Sunset Terrace. It wasn't big enough for both of us to fit in there at once, so she started handing out pots and pans for me to put into boxes in the living room.

When Mom had her head inside the cupboard I could say what I was really worried about, and feel like I was just talking to myself.

"It was weird there this afternoon," I said. "Bran was weird. He acted like—like he didn't want Mr. Marquis to see me. Like maybe he thought that if Mr. Marquis met me, he wouldn't want me living in the house. Bran didn't even let me introduce myself!"

Was I exaggerating? No, Bran had started talking even as I said "I'm Britt." I felt hurt all over again.

Mom popped her head out of the cupboard.

"Oh, honey," she said. "Did Bran really give you that impression?"

I nodded forlornly.

"Mr. Marquis knows I'm staying there too, doesn't he?" I asked. I had a sudden vision of Mom and Bran living happily in the house and me banished to, I don't know, maybe the shed in the back. I knew it was ridiculous, but I felt even more sorry for myself.

"Of course Mr. Marquis knows," Mom said. "But maybe . . ." She seemed to be choosing her words carefully. "Maybe the Marquises are feeling a little strange about this house-sitting deal. They've never had a house-sitter before, remember? Bran and I know you're mature and responsible and trustworthy. *I'd* trust you to take care of my house, if I had one. But maybe Bran thought Mr. Marquis would look at you and think, 'Oh, I didn't know she was such a little kid. What if she breaks something?' It's not your fault. It's just—this is kind of a weird situation."

"I'm twelve years old—almost thirteen," I said. "I'm not a little kid." I knew I was making myself sound like one, because my voice came out all whiny. "It's not my fault I'm small for my age." I was. I'd been the shortest kid in my class back in Pennsylvania, and I was the shortest kid in my class here in Florida. Come to think of it, that was probably one of the reasons I hadn't been any good at volleyball.

"I know," Mom said. "But Bran's sixteen, and I'm kind of surprised the Marquises would trust *him* with their house." She scrambled up from the floor, her buoyancy back. "Of course, I'm not about to tell the Marquises that. I wouldn't want to do anything to mess up this deal!"

She put the last pan in the box and sealed it with tape.

"Mr. Marquis thinks Bran is conscientious," I said, a little sulkily.

"He is," Mom said. "He's conscientious and responsible and mature beyond his years, because of the way he's had to grow up." She grimaced, and I knew she was thinking about Dad leaving us, and her having to work all the time, and Bran having to take care of me. Her grimace turned into a rueful smile. "He's much more trustworthy than *I* was at his age."

When Mom was sixteen, she eloped with my father. Her parents were so upset they disowned her.

I couldn't imagine Bran doing anything so bad that Mom

14

would disown him. I couldn't imagine him doing anything so bad she'd frown at him, even ever so slightly, the way she did at me when I forgot my homework or overslept or tracked in mud.

But I still thought Bran was up to something. Mom hadn't been there that afternoon. She hadn't seen how Bran was acting. And I hadn't done a very good job of describing it.

"Ready for bed?" Mom said. "I don't know about you, but I'm beat."

Mom went into the bathroom to brush her teeth. Then I helped her make up a bed on the couch where Bran would sleep when he got home from the restaurant. Back in Pennsylvania, the three of us always took turns sleeping on the couch. But ever since we'd gotten to Florida, Bran had insisted that Mom and I get the bedroom. It had something to do with the footsteps we sometimes heard racing past our door in the middle of the night. Once we'd even heard gunshots.

And I was worried about moving to the Marquises' house? Whatever Bran was up to, there couldn't be anything bad about getting away from Sunset Terrace.

3

We moved into the Marquises' house the day after school ended. It was only May, but the day was already roasting hot at 7:30 A.M. when Mom backed our car and the rented U-Haul into the Marquises' driveway. Mom hopped out and fanned her T-shirt back and forth to cool down.

"They do have air-conditioning, don't they?" I asked as I peeled the backs of my legs from the sticky vinyl seat.

Bran was busy unlocking the front door.

"Don't worry. It's already on," he said, and disappeared inside.

"I knew I liked these people," Mom said. She grabbed a box from the trunk and handed it to me. "Let's get this over with."

I walked up the Marquises' front walk—no, *our* front walk, I corrected myself. We'd never lived in a house before, and I felt downright extravagant having a front walk just for my family. For the summer, anyway.

Bran held the door open for me as he went back out for more boxes. I was hit by a wave of stale, warmish air. Where was that air-conditioning Bran had promised us?

Mom was right behind me, and she chuckled at my expression of dismay.

"Don't forget, the house has been shut up for a while," she said. She peered at a thermostat on the wall. "Just as I thought—it's set on eighty-two. We'll crank it up after we've got everything in."

It had been nearly a week since the Marquises left, and I guess it made sense that they wouldn't have kept heavy-duty air-conditioning on when no one was here. They'd said it was okay for Bran just to look in on the house occasionally until we could move in. I guess the greatest danger to the house was after school was out.

Mom put down her box and followed Bran back out to the car for more, but I couldn't help stopping to look around. My eyes took a minute to adjust fully to the dim room in front of me. It held two new-looking flowered green couches, a recliner, three coffee tables, a TV, a VCR/DVD player, a stereo, gold-framed pictures on the wall. . . . No wonder the Marquises were worried about something being stolen. They had a lot of things.

I set my box on top of Mom's and walked through the rest of the house, looking at everything. After the tiny apartment back at Sunset Terrace, this house seemed to go on and on. In one direction from the living room, there was a kitchen and a dining room and a laundry room and a sunroom and a screened-in porch. The bedrooms were in the other direction, down a long hall. There were three of them, all with double beds and wide chests and bureaus. The biggest bedroom even had a bathroom of its own.

Not only would none of us have to sleep on a couch in the living room, one of us wouldn't even have to share a bathroom.

"I feel rich," I said aloud. "I can't believe we're going to live here."

"Yeah?" Bran grunted, bringing in another box behind me.

"Well, rich girl, you forgot to hire movers. Guess you'll have to lower yourself to carrying your own boxes."

He handed me the box and I carried it on down the hall.

"Can I have the yellow room?" I asked. "You can have the blue one and Mom can have the one with the pink swirls."

"Doesn't matter to me," Bran said, turning back for more boxes.

By midmorning we were all soaked with sweat, but everything we owned had been transferred into the Marquises' house. It was strange to see our solid brown couch jammed in the sunroom with all the Marquises' white wicker furniture. Our kitchen table was folded up and hidden behind the couch. It had never hit me so strongly before that the table we'd eaten at and done our homework on for as long as I could remember was really just a flimsy card table, stored so easily. I felt like apologizing to all our possessions for shoving them aside and hiding them in out-of-the-way places, just because the Marquises' possessions were nicer. Every pot and pan and cup and glass we owned was going to stay boxed up all summer, because it made no sense to unpack our stuff when the Marquises' things were already on the shelves.

Thinking about glasses and cups reminded me how thirsty I was. I began opening cabinet doors in the kitchen, until I found a row of cups. I pulled one down, filled it from the faucet and gulped down the water. It had that same slightly seaweedy taste I'd never gotten used to back at Sunset Terrace. To distract myself, I studied the design on the cup, a strange plaid pattern of red and blue and yellow. I looked in the cupboards again—the plates were covered in the same design. Everything was an odd plastic that looked like it'd been around for decades. I turned over one of the plates and read the name on the bottom: Melmac.

"Hey, look at this," I called to Bran, who was stacking boxes in the laundry room. "How old do you think this is?"

Bran glanced my way but didn't answer.

"Know what I think?" I continued. "I bet they bought new dishes for their house up North and they brought all their old kitchen stuff down here. I bet this was the set of dishes they got as wedding presents or something. And they used it for years, up North, and now when they come to Florida and use it, it reminds them of being newlyweds, years and years and years ago."

I was having fun imagining the Marquises' lives, but all summer it was going to be strange eating off plates that were full of memories for people we didn't even know.

So silly of me—it wasn't like I hadn't been wearing second-hand clothes all my life. But this was different. The Marquises weren't done with these plates or their memories.

Suddenly I had Bran's attention.

"What are you talking about?" he asked.

I repeated my story. This time I added little flourishes: "They probably look at the little teeth marks on the cups and reminisce about when little Johnny got his first tooth—even though little Johnny's probably forty years old now. . . ."

"Jeez, Britt, you think these are antiques or something?" Bran asked. His voice didn't sound quite right. I figured he was straining to place a heavy box right at the top of a stack. But when I turned around, he wasn't even touching the boxes. He was staring at me and the plates.

"Antiques?" I said. I fingered the rim of the plate I was holding. It looked pretty cheap to me. If the Marquises really had gotten these dishes as wedding presents, they were gifts from their poor relatives. "No, I think they're just old."

"Still." Bran looked very worried. "I wouldn't want to break any of their dishes. Maybe we shouldn't use them. Why don't you pack all their kitchen supplies away right now, and we can use our own stuff all summer."

I looked at the open cabinet in front of me, full of glasses and dishes. It would take a good hour to empty just that cupboard. My shoulders already ached from carrying boxes. And I was so hot and tired I'd be more likely to break something trying to pack it now than I would using it for an entire summer.

"Nothing's going to get broken just sitting on that shelf," I said. "We can keep our stuff out on the counter. I can unpack that later."

"But—," Bran started to protest, just as Mom came walking toward the kitchen. He rushed past me. "Mom," he said in a complaining tone.

I stared after him. Bran didn't usually tattle. He usually just yelled at me himself.

But Bran wasn't saying anything about me. He was steering Mom away from the kitchen.

"Didn't the U-Haul guy say he'd give you a discount if we took the trailer back early?" he asked.

"Yep. And we've unloaded everything, so I'm ready to go. I was just making sure the AC was turned up before I left. Now that we're not coming in and out every five minutes, there's no reason to fry."

Mom was reaching for the thermostat on the living-room wall. Bran actually put his hand over the controls before she could touch it.

"We can't," he said. "I mean, I don't think the Marquises would want us to—"

"Bran." Mom almost laughed. "Don't be ridiculous. Surely the Marquises knew we couldn't leave the thermostat at eighty-two all summer. They just had it set there to keep things from getting moldy from the humidity while no one was here."

"Well, um—" Bran seemed stymied, but he didn't take his hand off the thermostat. "I just . . . I kind of promised them we wouldn't use a lot of electricity."

Mom backed away from the thermostat a little and peered at Bran.

"What exactly did you promise?" she asked. "Not to change the thermostat? Or just to do stuff like turning off lights when we're not using them?"

"Um, not to change the thermostat," Bran almost whispered. He didn't sound very sure of himself. "Not by much, I mean. We could probably go down to seventy-nine or so and it wouldn't matter."

Mom wiped the sweat off her forehead with the back of her hand. I could feel sweat trickling down my own face.

"What if we just offered to pay for the difference?" I asked.

Mom and Bran both just looked at me, and I knew what a stupid question that was. Air-conditioning was expensive. With Mom not working, we couldn't even afford 78-degree air.

"It doesn't really feel that hot in here," Bran said. "We'll be all right."

But his dark hair was plastered to his head with sweat. His face was so red he looked sunburnt.

I waited for Mom to tell him that he was crazy, that no one could survive in this heat. That the Marquises would have to be monsters to expect us to live in such a hot house all summer long. But Mom just stood there with her hair sticking up in sweaty clumps, tired wrinkles around her eyes. No, she looked more than tired. She looked scared.

Scared?

"I wouldn't want to do anything to mess up this deal," she'd told me that night when we were packing. Was she afraid that asking for a little cool air would make the Marquises change their minds, order us out, decide they didn't need house-sitters after all?

Would there be any moment the entire summer that we would be able to forget that we were living in somebody else's house?

"I guess people coped with a lot worse before air-conditioning was invented," Mom said. "Probably we should be glad to have air-conditioning at all."

"Right," Bran said, looking relieved. "Now, go on to the U-Haul place. Britt and I will unpack while you're gone."

I could tell that we were supposed to pretend, for the rest of the summer, that we didn't mind the heat. Bran and I were always pretending things like that: that we hadn't outgrown our shoes and didn't need new ones, that we didn't mind using the same backpack year after year after year for school, that we didn't want any of the toys or games we saw advertised on TV. Mom pretended too. She'd been pretending for years that she didn't mind working two jobs and struggling to pick up a college class or two here and there. I guess she'd minded a lot, if she was willing to live in an oven in order to go to school full-time.

But I was still hot. And cranky.

"Come on and help me in the kitchen," Bran said as soon as Mom left. "Hurry."

"No," I said. "I'm going to go unpack my room."

I deliberately turned my back on Bran and walked down the hot hall. Strangely, he didn't call after me, didn't order me to do what he said.

In a few minutes I almost forgot about him and the kitchen—even the heat—in the joy of getting to arrange a room that was going to be all mine, for the very first time in my entire life.

The yellow room, the one I'd picked, seemed to have been a spare bedroom. Several of the drawers in its white dresser were empty, or just partly filled with the kind of odds and ends people accumulate but can easily leave behind. One drawer held nothing but a plastic Winn-Dixie bag full of shells; another held a small collection of ceramic cats, most of them with broken tails. Had the Marquises had a cat? I brushed my hand over the tannish rug and came up with three orange-and-white hairs, roughly an inch long. Cat hair! I giggled, feeling like a brilliant detective.

I consolidated everything into the shell drawer—being careful not to break off any more of the ceramic cat tails—and then I had five drawers just for me. I put T-shirts in one, shorts in another, my brush and comb and ponytail rubber bands in the top. One of my blond hairs fell out of the brush and lay curled in the drawer. Somehow that pleased me. It was like proof that I'd been here, just like the cat.

"I do belong here," I said aloud, talking to myself in the mirror.

I pulled the prettiest of the ceramic cats out of the drawer and placed it on top of the dresser, decoratively angled in front of a crocheted Kleenex box cover.

"I claim you," I said. All summer long, it'd be like the ceramic cat belonged to me, not the Marquises.

Bran tapped at my door.

"Hey, Britt, is there anything in here that's breakable?" His eyes fell on the ceramic cat. "Let's wrap that up and put it away, okay?"

"But—," I said. My claiming of the cat had lasted exactly three minutes. "I won't break it. It's safe there."

"Accidents happen," Bran said. He plopped a box down on the floor and pulled a folded-up newspaper out from under his arm, where he'd been holding it. He ripped off a sheet of newspaper, stuffed the ceramic cat into the newspaper—rather roughly, I thought—and placed it down into his box. He started pulling out my drawers to look for more.

"Bran, that's *my* dresser," I complained. "You're invading my privacy." Which was kind of silly, because he, Mom, and I had shared a dresser until that very morning.

"It's the Marquises'," he grunted. He'd found the mother lode of ceramic cats and began shoving them into his box.

"Most of those are already broken," I said.

He shrugged. Finished with the cats, he shoved the drawer shut.

"What about the shells?" I taunted him. "They're breakable too. What if your irresponsible little sister picks one up and drops it and the pieces go all over the place? What if the Marquises fire you for that?"

"They're just shells," he said. "Plenty more of them on the beach." He glanced in my closet, pulled an ancient-looking quilt off the top shelf, then rushed out of the room.

"But what if these shells are special to the Marquises? What if they're irreplaceable?" I hollered after him. "And since when are quilts breakable?"

Bran didn't answer.

As far as I was concerned, he'd gone stark raving mad.

4

Mom brought back a frozen pizza for
us to have for dinner. When we baked it that night, we slid it
into the oven on our own familiar warped cookie sheet. I set the
table with our own familiar chipped plates and cracked plastic
cups, the ones that said, CROCKETT UNIVERSITY, PENNSYLVANIA'S
FINEST. It gave me a little lump in my throat to see them in the
Marquises' unfamiliar house.

But maybe the lump wasn't just from nostalgia. All of the
Marquises' kitchen supplies had disappeared—even the silverware. Whenever I opened a cabinet or pulled out a drawer, I
saw either our forlorn collection of utensils and plates and
cups, or bare wood. We didn't have nearly enough to fill the
Marquises' kitchen. Why had Bran made all that extra work for
himself, emptying drawers we didn't need? It made me feel like
he didn't trust me, like he was afraid I'd forget and use a Marquis
spoon by mistake. Did he really think I was such a little kid—like
some I'd baby-sat back in Pennsylvania—that I might destroy
everything in sight?

Why else would he have taken the ceramic cats out of my
room? Why else had he removed the quilt? Why hadn't he
taken the bed and the dresser and the crocheted Kleenex box
cover while he was at it?

I thought again about the first day Bran had showed me the

house, when he'd acted like he didn't even want Mr. Marquis to see me. What was wrong with me? What was wrong with Bran?

The buzzer went off, meaning the pizza was done. All three of us jumped.

Mom recovered first.

"We're pretty far gone, aren't we?" she laughed. "That's what moving will do to you. Now, where do the Marquises keep their hot pads?"

"Here," Bran said, reaching into a drawer beside the stove.

It was one of our hot pads he handed her, a red-and-green one I'd given Mom for Christmas a few years ago.

"You hid the Marquises' hot pads too?" I asked incredulously as Mom pulled the pizza out of the oven.

"I was afraid we'd get food on them or something," Bran said. "Like pizza sauce, maybe."

Did Mom hear how defensive he sounded, how un-Bran-like?

Mom was concentrating on cutting the pizza into slices.

"Pizza sauce would wash out," I said nastily.

"It might stain," Bran said. "I don't want to take any chances."

"I'm glad you're being careful," Mom said approvingly. "We wouldn't want to have to pay damages for anything." She put the pizza on the table and we all sat down. "That reminds me. Britt, I'm putting you in charge of laundry detail this summer. Bran, is there anything special she should know about the Marquises' washer and dryer? Isn't it great that we won't have to go to the Laundromat at all this summer?"

"Wait—we can't use their washer and dryer," Bran said

quickly. "The, um, Marquises said we weren't allowed."

"Oh," Mom said. She looked disappointed, but didn't say anything else.

She wasn't the one who was going to have to lug bags of dirty clothes to the Laundromat in 90-billion-degree heat.

"Why didn't the Marquises just put DON'T TOUCH signs everywhere?" I asked bitterly. "Or red velvet ropes, like at museums? Are we even allowed to breathe their air?"

"Now, Brittany," Mom said. "I know the circumstances aren't ideal, but remember—we're not paying to live here. They're paying us. So we can tolerate a few inconveniences, can't we?"

I shrugged, which wasn't how I usually acted to Mom. I felt ashamed, but I couldn't bring myself to apologize. We all chewed our pizza in silence for a few minutes.

"The Laundromat's just a few blocks away," Bran finally said, like he was trying to make up. "And there's a red wagon out in the shed that you can put the laundry in and pull it to the Laundromat. I can help you some of the time. It won't be too bad."

"So we're not allowed to touch the washer and dryer, but we can drag the Marquises' wagon all over town?" I asked. "That doesn't make any sense at all!"

"This is just what the Marquises want," Bran said through clenched teeth.

His face was red again, too red even for someone sitting in an overheated house. And he sounded . . . panicked. What did he have to be panicked about?

I looked over at Mom—would she finally, finally see that something strange was going on? But she wasn't looking at

Bran or me. Wasn't listening, either. She'd stopped chewing and was staring off into space. I could tell: Her body may have been with us, but her brain was already over at Gulfstone University.

If I complained again, Mom would just yell at me again. I looked away. My eyes focused on an odd rectangle on the wall, which was a darker shade of green than the rest of the wall. I squinted, confused. Hadn't there been a picture there only a couple of hours ago? Something old-fashioned-looking, like a dark vase filled with thorny flowers, I thought. I glanced around. All the walls I could see, in either the dining room or the living room, had those same darkened rectangles, where pictures had once hung. Panic started to rise out of my gut. Had thieves struck already, even as we were moving in? Then I realized what must have happened.

"Bran, did you hide all the Marquises' pictures, too?" I asked.

Bran nodded, looking down at his plate.

"I was afraid we might knock something down, moving," he mumbled. "And then I thought, we might as well leave them down for the rest of the summer. Just in case."

Mom was paying attention now. She laughed.

"Bran, I think the Marquises must have hired themselves the most conscientious house-sitter in the world," she said. "You are too much! What other sixteen-year-old boy would think of such a thing?"

Now it was Bran's turn to shrug, but his was the modest, "aw, shucks" kind.

I kept squinting. I was sure those pictures had been up there the whole time we were moving in. I was sure Bran hadn't taken them down until Mom left to return the U-Haul. But why? And why would Bran lie? He never lied.

Just then, the floor lamp by the front window clicked on, as if by magic. Bran jerked back in surprise, knocking his cup sideways. I caught it just in time to keep it from pouring Pepsi all over the Marquises' table and carpet. I looked around, hoping that Mom and Bran were impressed. I wanted them to say, "Good thing you're around to catch Bran's mistakes," or even, "Obviously Mr. Marquis was wrong about which kid was a danger to his possessions."

But Mom and Bran hadn't seen what I'd done. They were looking at the light, not me.

"Oh, it's on a timer," Mom said. "Bran, you didn't warn us about that one."

Bran was turned away from Mom, facing the light. Only I could see how perplexed he looked.

"They, uh, didn't warn me," he admitted. "And I've only been here during daylight the past week, so I never saw that light on—"

Mom walked over to the lamp and bent down to examine the timer attached to the lamp cord. So she probably couldn't tell how carefully Bran was choosing his words. His face looked like it always did back in Pennsylvania when we had to walk across the frozen puddles in the apartment-complex parking lot, never knowing when we'd break through the ice and get a bootful of muddy water.

"There," Mom said, pulling the timer off the lamp cord. "They won't need this to scare off thieves now that Bran Lassiter, champion house-sitter, is here!"

The lamp went dark again.

"Uh, Mom?" Bran said hesitantly. "Why don't you leave that on there? Just until I can talk to the Marquises and see what they want us to do."

Still squatting, Mom squinted back at Bran.

"I always heard that timers actually attracted thieves, clicking on and off at the same time every day. It's a dead giveaway. But—" She shrugged and replaced the timer. "This is your job, not mine. Just don't forget to ask them."

She came back to the table and took another piece of pizza. In a few minutes I could tell she was mentally back at Gulfstone University.

I looked from Mom to Bran, both now calmly chewing. I wanted to ask another question—if Bran was so worried about the air-conditioning using more electricity, why didn't he care about the lamp? What was going on? But I knew I wouldn't get a good answer. I kept my mouth shut and made a private vow. Bran didn't know it, but I was going to be watching him every bit as closely as he was watching out for this house.

5

We went to the beach the next day, Sunday. It was all of four blocks from the Marquises' house, so we walked, carrying lawn chairs and a picnic lunch. (Bran said the Marquises didn't mind us using their lawn chairs. Why could we drag their lawn chairs through sand and mud, but weren't even allowed to breathe near their pictures?) But Mom and Bran were both in festive moods, building sand castles and splashing in the water, so it was hard for me to remember I was supposed to be watching for Bran to act weird again. The three of us swam back and forth along the shore, and collapsed in giggles in the shallow water when Mom almost stepped on a crab, and practically did a flip into the water trying to avoid it. She surfaced with seaweed in her hair, and we laughed all the harder.

"This," she announced solemnly, "was worth moving to Florida for."

And then we all laughed again. She was right.

But on Monday, Bran went off to work at the Shrimp Shack, his other job, and Mom drove off for her first day of classes, and I was left alone. I washed the breakfast dishes—feeling almost as conscientious as Bran—and watched some TV. Ah, summer vacation. Only, I was thoroughly sick of commercials and fake laughter before it was even ten thirty. I flipped through the talk shows, where hunky actors and beautiful actresses talked about how hard they worked preparing for their roles. I didn't feel like watching Wile E. Coyote drop big rocks on Roadrunner. You know it's not worth watching TV when *Barney* is the best thing on.

What was I going to do with myself all summer?

Mom had been all for signing me up for some special program at the Y or someplace—until she saw the prices.

"They might have some financial aid available," she'd suggested, with a pained smile on her face. She flipped through the brochures I'd brought home from school, searching carefully.

"No, that's all right," I'd said. There probably was something in fine print about "help for children who couldn't afford our program otherwise." But I knew from experience: The people always treated you differently because of that. They talked slower to you and acted like you maybe weren't very bright just because you didn't have much money. I'd had enough of that back in Pennsylvania, surrounded by professors' kids. Now that we were in Florida and living in a nice house, I didn't want charity.

I decided to go back to the beach by myself.

Walking over there, I imagined meeting up with some other kids and having friends for the summer. We could gather at the beach every day, and go swimming, and visit back and forth at one another's houses. It had to be easier making friends at the beach than at school. To tell the truth, some of the kids at school had seemed a little scary. I was just as glad that Sunset Terrace was on the other side of Gulfstone from the Marquises' house.

I hit the beach trying to decide how to meet these wonderful friends. Should I play it cool for a while and wait until they invited me to join them? Or should I go right up to them and introduce myself? The second approach took more nerve, but I didn't want to waste the whole summer waiting.

The beach was empty.

Too late I remembered there had only been about four or five other people on the beach on Sunday, and all of them had had gray hair and wrinkles. It just hadn't mattered to me yesterday, because I'd had Bran and Mom. It had seemed nice then to have the beach mostly to ourselves. Now the whole place seemed lonely and ugly. I knew Gulfstone Beach wasn't exactly Florida's biggest attraction. I'd heard kids at school making fun of it. It had almost as much mud as sand, and the seaweed—or kelp, I didn't really know the difference—made swimming hard. But until today, it had seemed special. I'd always looked out at the waves lapping at the shore and marveled, "That's the Gulf of Mexico! I'm in Florida now!"

I was in Florida. So what?

Halfheartedly I walked along the water, feeling the sandy mud ooze between my toes. I poked holes in the sand and disturbed a crab that may have been the same one Mom almost stepped on the day before. Then I walked home.

It wasn't even quite noon yet, but the heat was already like a wall. The air was so thick I almost felt like I needed to swim through it. I looked around at the houses painted unnatural colors—baby blue, Pepto-Bismol pink, even an electric orange. None of the solid, ordinary browns and greens and whites like back in Pennsylvania. I felt like I was on a different planet. Suddenly I missed Pennsylvania and I missed Wendy and my other friends, and everything else we'd left behind.

I unlocked the door to the Marquises' house. After the heat outdoors, the minimal air-conditioning actually seemed cool. I sat down on the couch—the Marquises' couch—and discovered I even had goose bumps. But I didn't think that was just from the air-conditioning. It was because I felt so strange—strange and lonely and out of place. It was like I didn't even know who I was, alone in a stranger's house.

"I'm supposed to be here," I said aloud. "I have *permission*."

The blank squares on the wall looked back at me.

"The Marquises know I'm here," I told the squares, as if that were somehow in doubt.

I had goose bumps and now I was talking to a wall. I was really freaking out. I had to get a grip.

I went into the kitchen and made myself a peanut butter and jelly sandwich for lunch. I poured a glass of milk. I asked myself one of my favorite questions: What would Bran do?

"Bran doesn't get spooked," I told my sandwich. The sandwich didn't answer, which was a good thing—I hadn't gone totally loopy. But it seemed like what I said was wrong. The old Bran, the one I'd known all my life until we moved to Florida, didn't get spooked by anything. But the new Bran, the one who was house-sitting for the Marquises, was always jumpy, as jumpy as—my morning of TV viewing caught up with me—as jumpy as Scooby-Doo and Shaggy in a haunted mansion.

Haunted? Bran had certainly looked like he'd seen a ghost that first day when Mr. Marquis came out of the house, and on our moving day when I'd been talking about the Marquises' plates, and that evening when the lamp had switched on all by itself. But the Marquises weren't ghosts. They weren't even dead. They were just in New York.

I couldn't think about ghosts and the new, jumpy Bran right now. That made me feel weirder than ever. What would the old Bran do if he were me and he had a whole boring, lonely summer staring him in the face?

He'd do something to help Mom and me, I told myself. He always tried to do what was best for our family. And what did our family need right now? What did we always need?

Money.

Staring into my glass of milk, I felt like I'd been an idiot for not figuring this out sooner. Even the new, strange Bran was taking care of the Marquises' house *and* working at the Shrimp Shack. I felt selfish for worrying about what was on TV or how to make friends. I could get a job too. I'd just started baby-sitting before we left Pennsylvania. Why not here?

I crammed the last of my sandwich in my mouth, took a gulp of milk, and wiped the back of my hand quickly across my lips. A milk mustache wouldn't make a good impression. I stopped to run a comb through my hair, then raced out the door.

I let myself in at the gate of the house next door. Pots full of all sorts of unfamiliar tropical flowers blocked my path, but I ducked under hanging vines and dodged palm fronds and reached the front door.

And then I hesitated, my hand halfway up to the door. Remember how I said I wasn't any good talking to grown-ups? Mom or Bran had gotten me all my baby-sitting jobs back in Pennsylvania. I'd baby-sat for the kids of other waitresses, younger brothers and sisters of Bran's friends. I hadn't had to ask. What if everyone I talked to told me no? What if they said yes? What if they wanted references? What if someone actually hired me and I did a terrible job?

I was still standing there, frozen, when the door slowly creaked open.

"Were you going to knock or not?" an old lady in a huge, flowered dress asked me through the screen.

"I, uh, hadn't decided yet," I admitted.

"Life's too short to take a long time making decisions," the woman said in her strange, twangy voice. "Mine is, anyway. I guess I felt like I was going to live forever when I was your age."

What was I supposed to say to that?

"So if you'd knocked, what were you going to say?" the woman asked.

"I'm looking for a job," I mumbled. "Baby-sitting."

The old lady started laughing.

I felt the corners of my mouth turn down, on their own. If I didn't stop myself, I was going to cry.

The old lady stopped laughing.

"I'm sorry," she said. "It's just—there's not a little kid in this whole neighborhood. And no babies at all unless you walk clear on past the Winn-Dixie on the other side of the highway. You're going to have to get yourself another line of work."

I couldn't say anything, I was so busy fighting tears.

"Oh, come in, come in," the old lady urged. Her *come* sounded more like *Kim.* I didn't know what her accent was, but it made me have to listen harder just to figure out what she was saying.

"Now I feel like some lowdown snake, making a new friend cry," she continued. "'Least I can do is offer you some of my cinnamon jumbles."

I'd just met her and she was a billion years older than me and she was already calling me a friend? This wasn't what I'd

37

had in mind. But without thinking, I followed her into a dim living room crowded with more furniture than Mom, Bran, and I had in the Marquises' sunroom—with all of theirs plus all of ours. There were five end tables and two coffee tables, three couches, a love seat, and two recliners.

The old lady saw me looking at everything.

"Some of this is my son's. I'm just storing it for him for a while," she said. "Come on into the kitchen. We can breathe in there."

I threaded my way through the furniture, wondering how the old lady could squeeze by. She walked unsteadily, bending down to hold on to a chair's arm or a couch's back as she passed. I guessed the extra furniture kept her from having to use a cane.

In the kitchen, she leaned heavily against the counter, holding on all the way over to the refrigerator.

"Lemonade?" she asked.

I nodded uncomfortably. I knew Mom and Bran wouldn't approve of me being in a stranger's house. Back in Pennsylvania, I'd never seen the inside of any of our neighbors' apartments, unless I glanced in while walking by. And at Sunset Terrace, even glancing at a neighbor was probably like asking to be shot. But I couldn't see how this old lady could be a danger to me. She couldn't even walk on her own.

The old lady slid a plateful of thick, obviously homemade cookies onto a table covered in red-checked vinyl. Then she brought over a pitcher of lemonade and two glasses, before heaving herself into a chair. I sat down across from her.

"I'm Early Stuldy," she said. "I'll tell you that right off, so you can laugh if you want. Most people do."

She waited. I didn't laugh. She went on.

"Take yourself some of those jumbles," she said. "Go on. I baked them fresh this morning, 'fore it got too hot."

Hesitantly I slid one of the cinnamon-flecked cookies onto the empty plate at my place. The cookie was as big as the discus Bran threw on the track team. I took a bite.

"They're good," I said, really meaning it. I took another bite. "Delicious."

"My secret's the buttermilk," Mrs. Stuldy said. "People don't cook enough with buttermilk anymore. It's getting so it's hard to find. . . . Now, where did you say you lived?"

My mouth was full of cookie. I'd expected Mrs. Stuldy to keep talking about buttermilk. If I'd been Bran, I knew, I would have seen the question coming and waited to take another bite.

"Next door," I mumbled, trying to talk around the cookie.

"You're not one of the Wilders' grandkids, are you?" she asked. "No, Joyce told me they weren't coming down till next February."

"I live right over there." I pointed. I'd gotten turned around walking through Mrs. Stuldy's maze of living-room furniture, but I thought the Marquises' house was just on the other side of her kitchen wall. "My brother's house-sitting for the Marquises this summer, and my mom and I are living there too."

"Is that right?" Mrs. Stuldy said. Her eyes bugged out a little. "John and Mary didn't say anything about hiring a house-sitter. That's a little fancy for this neighborhood, don't you think?"

"I like this neighborhood," I said. "It's the nicest place I've ever lived."

"Well, me too, now I think of it," Mrs. Stuldy said. "House-sitters, though." She shook her head in wonder. "Makes me feel like I should be eating off fine china. Like in a soap opera. Usually John just hires someone to cut his lawn while they're away. One of those big corporations, you know? They come in their fancy vans and pull mowers off a big trailer—seems pretty silly for a yard like that, no bigger than a postage stamp. Roy, that's my husband, he's always telling John that we could take care of their yard for them, if they wanted. Since we're here year round, not having another house to go to. But John never wants to be beholden."

I hadn't quite followed all of that. But it bothered me how Mrs. Stuldy acted like she couldn't believe the Marquises would have hired house-sitters.

"My brother started mowing the Marquises' yard back in March," I said, a little shrilly. "He was so conscientious they decided to have him look after their whole house this summer."

Mrs. Stuldy nodded, accepting this.

"I've seen your brother, then, mowing," she said. "Tall fellow with dark hair? Good-looking?"

"That's him," I said, feeling proud that she thought Bran was good-looking. And feeling relieved, too, that this part of Bran's story checked out.

Why was I suddenly wondering if Bran had told the truth about anything?

"Mmm," Mrs. Stuldy said, still nodding. She poured lemonade for both of us and took a sip. "Well, then, you can probably solve a mystery for me."

"I can?" I said. I didn't feel like dealing with any more mysteries at the moment.

"I hope so," Mrs. Stuldy said. "See, Roy and me, a week ago

Saturday, we saw your brother putting boxes of something out in the Marquises' storage shed. Box after box after box . . . It looked kind of, well, suspicious, especially since we knew the Marquises had just left. Roy kept saying he was tempted to call the police. But I hate doing that if I don't *know* someone's guilty. Plus, it was broad daylight, and what kind of thief would try to steal things then? And it wasn't like your brother was taking the boxes away, he was just moving them around. And anyhow, we knew your brother had done work for the Marquises before. . . ."

Mrs. Stuldy kept looking over at me while she was talking, like she was expecting me to break in at any moment exclaiming, "Well, of course, Bran was doing that because—" But my brain was still stuck on some of the first words she'd spoken: *a week ago Saturday* . . . A week ago Saturday was the day Bran and I had come to the Marquises' house together. And then we'd left and Bran had gone into work at the Shrimp Shack, and Mom and I had started packing.

"Are you sure it wasn't this Saturday?" I asked Mrs. Stuldy. "Just two days ago, I mean—that's when we moved in."

"No," Mrs. Stuldy said. "It was a week ago. I know it was, because that was the night there was that poor motherless child on *Touched by an Angel*. My favorite TV show."

"Oh," I said, still puzzled. Would Bran have lied about going to work so he could come back to the Marquises' alone? Why?

Mrs. Stuldy was still looking at me, waiting.

"Well, I think I know what you saw Bran doing," I said slowly. I didn't want Mrs. Stuldy to think Bran was a thief. I may not have known what he was up to, but I *knew* he wouldn't steal anything. "Bran packed up some of the Marquises' belongings and put them into storage. To protect them, so we wouldn't break them or anything, living in the house. He packed up a lot more this past Saturday too, when we moved in. He's being extra careful with the Marquises' property."

"Oh," Mrs. Stuldy said. "But in the storage shed—you people aren't from around here, are you?"

"No," I said. "We just moved to Florida in February. From Pennsylvania."

"Then your brother probably doesn't know what the heat and humidity can do. You tell your brother to be sure he doesn't have any cloth or paper or pictures or anything like that out there in that storage shed, or by the end of the summer it could be rotted clear through."

"I'll tell him," I promised. "But I'm sure Bran knows already. I'm sure he was just doing what the Marquises told him to." I took a drink of my lemonade. It was as delicious as the cookies, but I couldn't quite enjoy it. "Your husband wouldn't have really called the police, would he?" I asked. "If you're still worried, you could call the Marquises. They'd tell you about us house-sitting. They'd tell you Bran wasn't doing anything wrong."

Why did I suddenly wish that she would call the Marquises? Why did I wish this old lady I'd just met would tell *me* that Bran wasn't doing anything wrong?

Mrs. Stuldy laughed, but it was different from when she laughed at me about baby-sitting. This laugh was rich and as sweet as the cookie I'd been eating. It was reassuring.

"Now, calm down, child," she said. "Roy talks about a lot of things he never has any intention of doing. And there's no need for anyone to go calling long-distance. Not with what that costs. I believe you." She chuckled, as if I'd told a particularly funny joke. "'Course I'm not going to call the Marquises. We'd look like a couple of busybody Nosy Nelly neighbors."

She was so amused it made me relax a little. I made a mental note to tell Bran and Mom about the funny way Mrs. Stuldy pronounced the Marquises' name. With her accent, it was almost *more kisses*. I remembered how the name had confused us the first night Bran had told us about his mowing job.

"Wait a minute—what'd you say?" Mom had interrupted as soon as Bran said his employer's name. "Marcus, like the boy's name?"

"Uh, no," Bran said. "Marquis. Like theater marquees. Or— isn't *marquis* a term for French nobility or something?"

"I guess," Mom said, and leaned back in her chair. She had a strange look on her face, but I'd thought it was just exhaustion. She'd worked a double shift waitressing that night.

Now, though, I wondered if I'd missed something. Bran had had a strange expression on his face too. I tried to remember: Was it that night or later, after the Marquises asked him to house-sit, that he told us how they spelled their name? I could remember seeing Bran write the name down for Mom, forming each letter carefully, dotting the *i* with great precision. Was that strange?

No. Bran did everything carefully and precisely.

But I didn't feel so relaxed anymore. Other questions crowded into my mind. Was Mrs. Stuldy confused about when she'd seen Bran with the boxes, or had he really started hiding them a week ago? Why? Why hadn't he told Mom and me what he was doing? And was Mrs. Stuldy still suspicious? What if she decided to call the police after all?

I took another bite of my cookie, and tried to study Mrs. Stuldy's face without her noticing. Her white hair stood out from her head in a way that reminded me of dandelion fuzz, and her skin was covered with age spots and wrinkles. But her eyes looked sharp and clear.

She caught me looking at her.

"Seeing as how we're neighbors now, and I'm feeding you cookies, and we've been talking for a while, isn't there something you should tell me, child?"

"Huh?" I said. What now?

"Your *name*," Mrs. Stuldy said. "You never did tell me your name."

She laughed again, and so did I. I was glad to get an easy question.

"Oh, sorry. It's Britt. Britt Lassiter. Well, really it's Brittany, but usually only my mom calls me that. Bran's name is short for Brandon—both of us kind of cut our names in half." I was rambling way too much because I was so relieved.

Mrs. Stuldy didn't seem to notice. She took a sip of her lemonade.

"Brittany and Brandon—those certainly are pretty-sounding. People give their children such fancy names nowadays."

"Yes, ma'am. That's why my mom gets upset at Bran and me for not using our full names. She says she searched the baby name books for months to come up with the right names. She's given up on Bran—even she calls him that. But she's still got hope she can talk me into *Brittany*."

I remembered overhearing Mom once, back in Pennsylvania, telling her friend Carlene, "It's bad enough I'm raising them in a broken home. But they've got broken names,

44

too. Sometimes it hurts just to hear that. Britt and Bran. Bran and Britt."

"Sounds like some sort of health food," Carlene had said. "Some cereal old people eat so they don't have to take Metamucil."

And then she'd snickered in a mean way. They were in the kitchen and I was in the living room—it was my turn on the couch that night—and I'm sure Mom thought I was asleep or she wouldn't have said that. So I couldn't protest. But it bothered me. How could she say we had a broken home? I thought it was just fine. A lot of the kids I'd known at school, even the ones who lived with both their mom and their dad, had a lot more problems than Mom and Bran and me. Why didn't my mother understand that I liked *Britt* better than *Brittany* because there were two other Brittanys in my class, and I wanted to be different?

Mrs. Stuldy was nodding, as if she at least understood me.

"Oh yes. Kids always want to go their own way. And parents mostly have a hard time letting them go."

She looked so sad all of a sudden, I was afraid she was going to cry.

"What's wrong?" I asked awkwardly.

She let out a heavy sigh.

"Oh, it's a long story you probably don't have time for." She took a long drink of her lemonade. I wasn't sure what to say. We just sat there eating and drinking in silence, and then Mrs. Stuldy said, "Well, I shouldn't keep you from your job search. You've got a long way to go to find someone with young children."

"Do you know anyone in particular who might need some

help?" I asked. I didn't feel like knocking on a lot of strange doors.

"Not with little kids, I sure don't," she said, shaking her head sadly. Then she kind of gasped, and her whole face lit up. "Why, I have an idea! If you want some work, it doesn't have to be baby-sitting, does it? I know just what you can do around here. How are you at running errands?"

"Well, I—," I started to answer, but Mrs. Stuldy was so swept away with her idea she just kept talking.

"This isn't anything hard," she said. "I just know the Harrisons, over on the next corner, are always looking for someone to pick up their prescriptions for them, and Mrs. Zendt always runs out of milk right at supper time—she never remembers to pick it up when her daughter takes her shopping—and I really would like to see the latest issue of *People*. You know, that nice man in the wheelchair who used to be Superman is on the cover. But I forgot and let my subscription run out. And since I had this hip replacement surgery, I haven't been able to get out much—"

"I'm not old enough to drive," I said.

Mrs. Stuldy waved that worry aside.

"Oh, you can walk to everything," she said. "That's why we all moved down here, thinking we could just walk to the beach and walk to the store and walk to the bus stop when we all got too old to drive. None of us thought the first thing we'd lose would be the ability to walk!"

And then she laughed, as if it were all a big joke.

"Where do you want me to get your *People*?" I asked, standing up.

By the end of the day, I'd delivered medicine to the

Harrisons, milk *and* flour to Mrs. Zendt (you try lugging a gallon carton and a ten-pound bag five blocks in 90-degree heat!), and *People* and earwax drops to Mrs. Stuldy. And I had four requests from some of Mrs. Stuldy's other friends for me to run some errands the next day. One woman, Mrs. Tibbetts, even wanted to know if I could pick up the *National Enquirer* for her every week.

I was so busy I didn't have time to think about Bran acting weird or moving boxes, or Mr. Stuldy almost calling the police on him, or me having to sit alone in a strange house all summer long.

But it all came back to me when I limped back to the Marquises' house at five o'clock clutching a wad of dollar bills. I let myself in the front door and just stood there, leaning against the wall, inhaling the almost cool air. I tried to decide what I was going to tell Mom and Bran about my day. The money in my hand seemed to give me power. I decided I'd start with, "Let's go to Burger King! My treat!"

And maybe, sitting on plastic chairs in that brightly lit restaurant, eating burgers and fries that tasted the same in Florida as they did back in Pennsylvania, Bran would stop acting weird. Maybe he would explain why he'd lied about going to work last Saturday (if he had), why he'd been so fanatical about packing away the Marquises' things, why he'd been so nervous around Mr. Marquis that first day. Probably he had a perfectly reasonable explanation for everything.

I just couldn't imagine what it would be.

6

Nothing went as I'd planned that evening.

First of all, I couldn't treat us all to Burger King because Bran came home from the Shrimp Shack with three white foam boxes of seafood and pasta and salad and bread.

"Lunch leftovers," he explained. "They throw it out if none of the employees want it. So we're going to be feasting all summer long!"

I peeked into the top box in the refrigerator with mixed feelings. I couldn't keep my mouth from watering at the sight of the shrimp and scallops and crabmeat swimming in Alfredo sauce—back in Pennsylvania seafood like that was such a luxury I'd only tasted it once or twice in my entire life. I'd take scallops over Burger King any day. But I felt outdone by Bran once again. I had blisters on my feet from walking back and forth between the drugstore and the grocery store and this neighborhood all afternoon, and all I had to show for it was thirteen dollars. (Mrs. Stuldy had told me to charge four dollars per errand, but then she gave a dollar tip.) Bran was getting paid for a whole day's work, and he'd gotten us dinner just by saying, "No, don't throw that in the trash. I'll take it." Not to mention he was providing us with a place to live, by house-sitting for the Marquises.

Was I jealous? Was that all? And was I just imagining that

Bran was acting weird because he was doing so much for our family and I was just me—Britt Lassiter, an okay kid, but nobody special?

I shut the refrigerator a little too hard and it shook. I waited for Bran to yell at me for abusing the Marquises' precious possessions. But he just glanced up from setting the table.

"Hard day, Britt?" he said with real sympathy.

It's really hard to feel jealous of someone as nice as Bran. But I was still suspicious.

Mom came in just then, saw the nearly set table and cried out, "Oh, you two are the greatest! I'm starved. I never knew thinking could make someone so hungry."

"How was school, Mom?" I asked, putting out paper napkins.

"Oh, wonderful," she said. "I know, I know, you guys go to school all the time, but you can't imagine how great it feels to me to just focus on learning all day long. Did you know that everyone begins as something called a zygote? And that for the first eight weeks, a human embryo doesn't look any different from a pig's or a goat's? Isn't that interesting? It seemed like everything I heard today was like that—incredible and amazing and wonderful, and I'm so happy!" She twirled in the middle of the kitchen. "I've had brainless jobs for so long that it's like my brain has just been starving for this. But I've got so much work to do now, I'm going to be up until midnight just reading the first assignments. . . . How'd you guys do today?"

"All right," Bran said. "The Shrimp Shack is Brainless Job Central. But it's a nice break from school." I could tell he hurried to add that so Mom wouldn't feel guilty.

"I had an interesting day," I said.

But we were all scrambling to get the food heated up and on the table, so I didn't explain. I listened to Mom talk some more about embryology, and Bran told about a Shrimp Shack customer who ate eighty-four fried scallops and two servings of fries. I waited until we'd gobbled down all the pasta and seafood and sopped up all the Alfredo sauce with the bread.

"Anyone feel like ice cream?" I asked when we were all leaning back contentedly in our chairs. "My treat."

Mom and Bran both turned to me with questioning looks on their faces, just as I expected.

"I got a job," I announced proudly, and waited for their congratulations.

But they didn't react right after that. First Mom said, "Oh, Brittany, I hope you don't feel like you have to work because I'm not supporting us well enough. You're only twelve. You should be thinking about fun, not money."

"But it was fun, and anyhow, there's nothing else to do around here—" That didn't sound right.

Mom looked troubled, but asked, "What's your job?"

I explained. Then it was Bran who got all upset.

"You talked to the neighbors?" he asked. "I mean, we don't even know these people. You shouldn't go into strangers' houses."

"But it wasn't dangerous," I said. "And how did you get your mowing job and your house-sitting job and, and even your restaurant job—except from talking to strangers?"

"That's different," Bran said.

"He's not a twelve-year-old girl," Mom said.

I couldn't believe Bran and Mom weren't as happy as I was about my new job. I thought they'd be proud of me.

"But everybody was really nice," I argued. "And anyhow,

these people are old. They couldn't hurt me if they wanted to. Mr. Harrison can't even get out of his wheelchair."

"Still," Bran said sternly. "Mom, tell her she has to stay away from the neighbors." His voice was strange, almost panicky.

Mom had her head tilted to the side, considering.

"Mom!" I protested. I had wanted to wait to bring up everything Mrs. Stuldy'd told me. But I knew it was my best ammunition. "If I hadn't met Mrs. Stuldy, she might have called the police on Bran, because she and her husband saw him moving boxes around, and they were suspicious. And the Marquises never told them that Bran was house-sitting, so the Stuldys would have been really suspicious when they saw us going in and out of the house. And, Bran, did you start moving the Marquises' things around a whole week ago? The same day you showed me the house?"

For a minute, Mom and Bran just stared at me.

"The police?" Mom sounded stunned. "Oh, no. Bran, did the Marquises give you anything like a signed contract that you could show if anyone questioned our right to be here?"

"I'll talk to them about that," Bran mumbled, looking down.

"Well, even if the police came, everything would be straightened out as soon as they talked to the Marquises," Mom said. "But it would be a big hassle, especially if they couldn't reach the Marquises right away."

Bran was still looking down. He hadn't answered my other questions.

"Did you come back last Saturday and start packing up the Marquises' stuff?" I demanded.

"Uh, yeah, I did," he admitted.

"But you told Mom and me you went to work at the Shrimp Shack."

"I came here on my way to work," Bran said quickly. "I wasn't *lying*."

Well, maybe not. But the Shrimp Shack was between the Marquises' house and Sunset Terrace. He'd gone a long way out of his way to get here. And why? Why had he been so eager to move things right away?

"What all did you put out in the storage shed, anyway?" I asked.

"Just stuff," Bran said. "What is this, the Inquisition?"

"Mrs. Stuldy, she said you had to be careful, that since we haven't lived here for very long, we don't know what the heat and humidity can do. She said if you put any paper or fabric or pictures out there, they'd be rotted clear through by the end of the summer."

"Oh, dear," Mom said. She sounded almost as worried as she'd been about the police. "And you were trying to be so careful, Bran. Is there anything out there that might be damaged? If you want, you can move some of the boxes into my room. I have a lot more space than I need. And Brittany and I can help—"

Bran was already shaking his head.

"No!" he burst out. "I can take care of everything myself!"

The old Bran, the one I'd known all my life, never would have interrupted Mom like that. He never would have used that nasty tone with her—or anyone.

"I mean, I don't want you to take any time away from studying, Mom," Bran said, sounding a little calmer. "And Brittany, she might break something—"

"I would not!" I said.

I glared at him. He seemed to back down a little.

"Well, anyhow, the boxes aren't the problem," Bran said. "It's Brittany going around all over the neighborhood, talking to everyone—Britt, you can't do that again. You're lucky nothing happened today. Maybe none of these people look dangerous but you don't know. . . . Mom, weren't you going to sign her up for a day program at the Y or something? She needs to be around young people, kids. Not some old people we don't even know."

I hated it when Bran talked to Mom as if I weren't even there. And why was he more worried about old people we didn't know than young people we didn't know?

"Mo-om," I appealed. "I don't want to go to the Y. I want to keep working. I like our neighbors. Isn't it good to want to help them? Isn't it good that Mrs. Stuldy *won't* call the police on us because she knows me now?"

I couldn't help shooting a nasty look toward Bran. He looked pale. And I thought he'd gotten really tan at the beach the day before.

Mom rubbed her temples as if she were thinking hard. Then she looked up and began speaking slowly. I could tell she was figuring things out as she went.

"Maybe I overreacted a little, Brittany, because I feel guilty that I'm not working this summer. I don't see anything wrong with you making a little extra money. I should be glad you want to work." She glanced at Bran. "But Bran's right to be cautious about strangers. Maybe I should go and meet all the people you're going to run errands for, to make sure you're safe."

"No, I'll do it," Bran said quickly. "Remember, you've got all that work to do for college."

Mom looked at him doubtfully for a minute, then shrugged.

"Overprotective Bran strikes again," she muttered. "Guess we'll all have to work together to make sure I get this scholarship. All right, Bran, you are hereby deputized to check out Brittany's customers. Now, is everybody happy?"

Bran and I both nodded. But we didn't go out for ice cream. I didn't feel much like celebrating anymore, knowing Bran wanted to end my errand business after one day. And knowing that the news about my job had made him act weirder than ever. Why was Bran so paranoid about the neighbors? Why was he so defensive about those stupid boxes in the shed?

7

Bran disappeared right after dinner. Mom settled in at the table doing homework, so I knew I couldn't turn on the TV and bother her. I drifted through the house, then out to the backyard.

The storage shed gleamed in the light from the setting sun. It was a small tan building, kind of a miniature barn. I knew the lawn mower was in there, because I hadn't seen it anywhere else. Allowing for a few gardening tools and whatever else people usually kept in sheds, that left maybe five or six square feet for boxes. Or cubic feet, I guess—wasn't that the right name for when you included height, too? How many boxes could fit in that space?

I slipped across the yard. It wasn't like I really meant to open the door and search the shed, but I was still disappointed when I reached out and touched the door latch. A big, fat padlock held it shut.

Well, naturally. I knew Bran wouldn't leave the Marquises' precious possessions out in an unlocked shed, ready for anyone to take. But somehow I'd thought . . .

I didn't know what I'd thought. I felt kind of light-headed from the heat and my long day of walking and the argument with Bran.

I pulled one of the Marquises' chaise lounge lawn chairs out of the sunporch and sat down, facing the storage shed. I watched through the palm fronds as the sun set the rest of the way. And then I just sat and waited, like a guard dog. Except I didn't know what I was waiting for.

Or what I was guarding.

The streetlights clicked on, sending a dim glow into the back-yard. I lay back on the chaise lounge. It was finally a pleasant temperature outdoors—not too hot, not too cold, not too sticky. I closed my eyes, savoring the strange feeling of not having sweat running down my body. And then I must have fallen asleep, because the next thing I knew, I was jolting awake.

For a few minutes, I just lay still, trying to remember where I was and why I was there. And trying to figure out what time it was. I glanced behind me—all the windows in our house were pitch black. The windows of the Stuldys' house were dark too. The moon was high in the sky—it had to be the middle of the night.

Feeling totally disoriented, I sat up—and gasped. I suddenly knew what had awakened me.

A shadowy figure had just finished unlocking the door of the shed and was stepping inside.

I blinked. The figure was out of my sight now. Had I imagined the whole thing?

No, the door was definitely open. It creaked a little, swinging in the breeze. Why was the shed door open in the middle of the night?

I slid off the chair and tiptoed over to the shed. Mom and Bran would be so proud of me if I stopped a thief.

Or would they be furious with me for not running inside and calling 911 right away?

I kept moving toward the shed. I'd feel like a fool calling the police or waking Mom and Bran if the whole thing was just a figment of my imagination. Or if there was some perfectly reasonable explanation for the shed being open—even though I couldn't think of one. I pressed my back against the wall of the shed and peeked into the open doorway. It was hard to see in such dim light, but the figure was bent down over a box, using a small flashlight to peer inside. Some of the flashlight's glow reflected back on his face.

It wasn't a thief. It was my brother.

"Bran! What are you doing?" I shrieked.

He dropped the flashlight and it rolled toward me. I picked it up.

"Jeez, Britt, you scared me to death," Bran said, jerking the flashlight out of my hand. He shone it right into my face, like I was a suspect caught in a crime. "What are you doing out here?"

"I—," I started.

"Ssh! You're going to wake up the whole neighborhood," Bran said crossly. "Why aren't you in bed?"

"I fell asleep in the lawn chair," I said, keeping my voice low. "I woke up when you opened the shed."

"The lawn chair? Outside? Why?" Bran asked.

"I didn't mean to," I said. "I was just tired."

"Mom and I thought you'd gone to bed early," Bran said. He still sounded cross. "Your door was shut."

Didn't Mom think I would have said good night to her? I wondered. Or had she been too busy studying to notice?

"Anyhow, you should be in bed now, " Bran said sternly. "Go on."

I didn't go.

"Why aren't *you* in bed?" I asked. "It's got to be the middle of the night. What are you doing?"

"I'm checking to make sure there's nothing out here that could rot," Bran said. "Remember? You were so worried?"

His voice wasn't just cross or stern now—it was mean. He was mad at me, and I didn't know why. And because he was shining the flashlight at me, I couldn't see his face to try to gauge what he was really thinking.

"But—why are you doing that now?" I asked. "Why didn't you do it right after dinner?"

"I had other things I had to do then," Bran said. "All right?"

I tried to look past Bran, past the flashlight, to see the mysterious boxes. But they were just shadowy shapes in the dark of the shed.

"I could help you," I said. "I wouldn't break anything. I promise."

"No, you need your sleep," Bran said. "Come on. I'll take you inside."

And then he took my arm and actually escorted me across the yard and into the house. The digital clock on the VCR glowed red numbers at us: one, two, one, five. It was twelve fifteen, just after midnight. (And why hadn't Bran hidden the VCR away too, if he was scared of things being broken?)

"You'll be okay now," Bran said, as if I'd been in some great danger out in the backyard. "Just go back to sleep."

I went into my room and lay down on my bed, but I wasn't sleepy anymore. I felt too strange. I got up again and pressed my ear against the door. Every ten minutes or so, I could hear Bran's footsteps out in the hall, tiptoeing to and from his room.

He's moving boxes again, I thought. *He's moving them into his room.*

And that made me happy. Not for any good reason—not because I was relieved that the Marquises' possessions would be protected from mold and rot. No, I was happy because Bran's room didn't have a lock on the door.

I could look in the boxes if they were in Bran's room.

8

When I woke up the next morning I was still slumped against the door. I'd spent part of the night on a lawn chair and the rest sleeping on the floor—no wonder I felt so groggy.

The sunshine was bright outside my window, and some sort of birds were singing in the palm trees. My window looked out on a huge bush of a kind of exotic flower I'd never seen back in Pennsylvania. It had an exotic name, too—bird of paradise, I think.

With all the sunshine and birds and flowers, it seemed like I'd just had a bad dream the night before. Everything always seems more innocent in daylight than in darkness. Maybe I'd imagined the panic in Bran's voice when I found him in the shed, the way he seemed to want so desperately to keep me from seeing the boxes. Maybe it wasn't so strange that he'd waited until twelve fifteen, when Mom and I were both supposed to be asleep, before he'd opened the shed.

I stumbled out of my room and down the hall to the kitchen. Bran was sitting at the table, eating a bowl of cereal and glancing through the mail. When he saw me coming, he ripped a page out of the Eckerd's sale circular and tucked it in his pants pocket.

I hadn't imagined anything the night before. He was still

acting strange. He was acting . . . guilty.

"Is Eckerd's having a big sale?" I asked. "You interested in buying two-for-one Fibercon?"

He looked over at me like he was trying to pretend that he hadn't seen me come into the kitchen.

"Batteries," he said, not very smoothly. "They have, uh, Energizer batteries really cheap, and I'm taking the page with me so I remember to pick some up."

He was lying. It was so obvious I could hardly stand it.

"Let me see," I said, holding out my hand.

"Brittany, I'm trying to eat," he protested.

As if he couldn't chew and reach into his pocket at the same time.

"Hey, I could get the batteries for you," I said. "I'll probably be running errands at Eckerd's today anyway."

"*If* all your customers check out," Bran said, and he had the upper hand again.

I poured some Cheerios for myself.

"Did Mom leave already?" I asked.

"At the crack of dawn," Bran said, in a way that made me feel guilty for sleeping late.

We ate the rest of our breakfast in silence.

After we'd both taken showers and gotten ready, we walked over to Mrs. Stuldy's together. Bran wasn't acting weird anymore, but I felt like I had my own personal storm cloud beside me.

It was one thing to try to catch him in a lie at breakfast, when it was just the two of us. It was another thing to show him off to our new neighbor and have him seem so gloomy.

"Come on, Bran," I said. "I told her I had a nice family. She's going to take one look at your face and think I was lying. You look as grumpy as Eeyore."

Bran stopped frowning long enough to look puzzled.

"Eeyore?"

"You know, from Winnie the Pooh? The donkey that's always totally miserable?" I made my voice as sad and mopey as Eeyore's, and Bran rewarded me with a snort that could have turned into a laugh.

"Sorry," he said, sounding more like his usual self. "I'm just worried. About you, I mean."

And then he put his arm around my shoulder and gave me a little hug. My friend Wendy back in Pennsylvania used to go crazy when she saw Bran do something like that.

"You realize how incredible that is, don't you?" she asked once. "Sixteen-year-old boys, as a rule, are not nice to their sisters. They don't even want to be in the same room with them, let alone give them comforting hugs."

Wendy's mom was a psychology professor who specialized in adolescent behavior, so she should have known. But I only had experience with one brother, Bran, and he'd always been nice to me. That's why his strange behavior now really bothered me.

Bran took his arm off my shoulder to ring Mrs. Stuldy's doorbell.

"I think you could run your errands as long as you don't actually go into the people's houses," Bran said. "And you shouldn't talk to them any more than you have to. You're running a business, right? You don't have time for socializing."

"Who's there?" Mrs. Stuldy hollered from inside.

"It's Britt from next door," I yelled back. "And my brother's with me."

"Come in! It's open!" Mrs. Stuldy yelled again. "I'm back in the kitchen!"

I looked at Bran and he looked at me. I could see he wasn't happy, but we pushed our way in. Bran silently followed me through the maze of furniture in the living room.

The kitchen smelled like cinnamon and yeast, and I quickly saw the reason why. Mrs. Stuldy was sliding a freshly baked coffee cake onto the table.

"Oh, I thought you'd be back today," she said, sounding pleased. "Sit down, sit down. You can join me for a piece of cake, can't you? I remember from when my son was little—kids your age are always hungry."

"Thank you," Bran said politely as she cut a piece for him. But I'd never heard him sound more miserable.

"Bran was worried," I said. "He wants to meet all the people I'm going to be running errands for, just to make sure there's no one, uh, dangerous."

In Mrs. Stuldy's sunny kitchen, the notion seemed crazier than ever. But Mrs. Stuldy didn't take offense.

"Oh, it's true, you can never be too careful," she said sadly.

She started struggling to get up. Bran noticed and asked quickly, "Can I get something for you?"

"Why, yes," she said. "I was just going to bring over the pot of tea—"

Bran rushed to get it from the counter, and poured tea for us all.

"Thank you," she said. "What a nice young man."

Bran looked down at his coffee cake, missing the bright smile Mrs. Stuldy directed his way. She was wearing a nicer dress than the day before—the flowers were smaller and more subtle, on a blue background, instead of gaudy orange. Her hair was neatly combed, and she'd put a wavering line of lipstick around her mouth. Had she gotten dressed up because of me? I'd never thought much about it before, but I wondered suddenly what it would be like to have someone like Mrs. Stuldy as my grandmother—someone who baked cookies and cakes and smiled admiringly at everything I said. I was sure Mrs. Stuldy had about a dozen grandkids and treated them all like kings and queens. It didn't seem fair, suddenly, that my own grandmother was a thin, fussy woman who had snapped, "Don't touch my dress with those dirty hands!" the only time I'd ever met her. That was when I was five. I guessed I had another grandmother too, but it was hard to count someone who didn't even know I was alive.

I took a big sip of my tea and burned my tongue. Even Bran grimaced a little as he swallowed.

"I, uh, understand that the Marquises forgot to tell you they'd hired me to house-sit," he said, putting down the cup. "I tried to call them last night, to find out if there was anyone else who might be surprised about us living there, but I couldn't reach them. So do you know—?"

Bran let the question hang in the air. Mrs. Stuldy blinked a few times, like she wasn't sure what he was asking. What if Bran thought she was dangerous because she got confused?

"He means he doesn't want anyone thinking they should call the police on us," I said, laughing a little to make it sound like a joke. "Are there any other neighbors who might see us at the house and think we're thieves—when we're actually the ones trying to *protect* the house from thieves?"

Mrs. Stuldy tilted her head to one side, considering.

"Why, I don't *think* so," she said. "The Marquises weren't the types to be buddy-buddy with everyone. They kept to themselves, you know."

"But the other neighbors—" Bran guided her back to his question.

"Well, now, let's see, Mrs. Shoemaker, over on the other side of you, she's blind, so she couldn't hardly be watching the house, could she? And the Joynowitzes and the Pauleys and the Romans across the street, they all went back North themselves a month or so ago—" She seemed about to list everyone in the neighborhood, but then she stopped. "Oh, that reminds me. I thought of some more customers for you. I wrote down their names and numbers."

She handed me a sheet of paper covered in shaky writing. I held it out so Bran could see.

Bran sighed and looked at his watch.

"Britt, don't you think we should be going?" he asked.

I looked longingly at the coffee cake. I would have liked another piece. And Mrs. Stuldy looked so disappointed all of a sudden.

"I need to meet these other people before I go in to work," Bran explained.

"I'll come back later," I promised Mrs. Stuldy.

Her face brightened, just as Bran began glowering again.

It took us a half an hour, flat, to go through the list of people I might be running errands for. For the first couple of people, the ones nearest Mrs. Stuldy's house, Bran carefully explained about how he was house-sitting for the Marquises, and I was helping out. But once we got to the next street over, I noticed that Bran didn't even bother giving his name. I thought it was funny—some of the people were so concerned about their own safety that they didn't even unhook their chains to talk to us. Others could barely walk to the door. I wondered how they could possibly be any danger to me. At the end, I asked Bran, "So, are you convinced now?"

"I guess it's okay," Bran said with another sigh. "But don't talk too much to these people. Don't tell anyone else where you live, and—"

"Why not?" I asked. I suddenly had to take big steps on the cracked sidewalk to keep up with him.

"Think about it," Bran said with a frown. "Remember? You're going to be at home by yourself a lot of the time. You need to be safe."

I frowned too, but didn't argue.

"So don't talk about Mom or me, or tell them where we are or when we're away," Bran continued. "And don't go into anyone else's house. I mean it."

I wondered why Bran didn't chain me to the Marquises' house and be done with it.

"Not even Mrs. Stuldy's?" I asked. "Come on—you don't seriously think she could be dangerous. It would hurt her feelings if I didn't visit some."

Bran's frown deepened, if that was possible.

"Okay, okay." He gave in. "Just—be careful. Don't talk too much. Don't bother her."

That hurt, and I didn't understand. Why was talking a problem? Mrs. Stuldy acted like she was desperate for someone to talk with. Maybe Bran just meant I shouldn't do all the talking; I should let her have a turn. What kind of an inconsiderate brat did he think I was?

We were back at the Marquises' house—our house—now, and Bran rushed on inside without looking back to see if I followed. I sat down on the front porch—it was just a small concrete square, raised a foot off the ground. Some sort of lizard scuttled up the walk beside me, and I gasped. It was the kind of animal I was used to seeing in zoos, not on my front porch.

"Hey, Bran!" I yelled. "Come and look!"

Bran poked his head out the door.

"Uh-huh. Cool," he said, without really looking at the lizard. He looked up and down the deserted street. "Now come on in. You shouldn't be out on the front porch."

I was too stunned to protest as he actually took my arm and pulled me inside.

I didn't understand this, either.

"What's wrong with sitting on the front porch?" I demanded when the door shut behind us.

Bran wouldn't look at me.

"You know, it makes a place look trashy to have a lot of people out front. I'm supposed to be keeping this place looking nice. Just stay out of the front."

Then he turned and headed for his bedroom.

I was left speechless. Since when was I "a lot of people"? And wouldn't the Marquises *want* us to be out front, so people driving by could see that the house was occupied? But one look at the set of Bran's shoulders as he walked away from me convinced me it wasn't worth asking him anything.

Whatever was in the hidden boxes would have to be pretty impressive if they were going to answer all the questions swarming in my mind.

9

Bran left for work at one o'clock, right after lunch.

I waited long enough to watch him take off on his bike. And then, at precisely 1:01, I tiptoed down the hall to his room.

The door was shut but I pushed it open. If he came back now I could say, "Oh, Bran, hi. I was just checking to see if you had a . . ." I couldn't think what I might be checking for, what I might legitimately be planning to borrow.

Bran didn't come back. I stepped into his room.

Bran had made his bed, very neatly, and he'd stacked his books on the dresser with almost military precision. His room, like mine, appeared to have been a guestroom for the Marquises, and Bran seemed to be treating it like he was just a visitor—a very polite one. (I thought guiltily about the tangle of sheets I'd left strewn across my bed, the dirty clothes I'd left on my floor.) But I already knew Bran was much neater than I was. I was looking for boxes.

There weren't any lying around on the floor or under the bed, so I made a beeline for the closet. I practically held my breath as I reached out for the doorknob.

It wouldn't turn. It was locked.

I jerked my hand back as if the doorknob had burned me. Locked? How could that be?

I bent down and examined the doorknob carefully, as if it were a clue. I remembered all those TV police shows where the experts pick up a nearly microscopic scrap of paper with tweezers, and that solves the whole case for them. I wanted that kind of evidence. But this was just an ordinary doorknob, rounded and shiny. Almost too shiny . . .

I stepped away from the doorknob and went back to the main door of Bran's room. I looked at it, felt its doorknob. Then I looked at the doorknobs to my room and Mom's, and to all the other closets in the house. None of them were shiny. None of them had locks on them. Why would the Marquises have a door that locked on a guestroom closet but not anywhere else?

I went back into Bran's room and looked at the closet doorknob again. Compared with the other doorknobs, this one looked different. It looked . . . newer. Maybe even brand-new.

I tried opening the doorknob once more, hopelessly. And then I just backed away and sat down on the bed.

I didn't have any proof, but I was pretty sure that that doorknob hadn't belonged to the Marquises. Bran had bought it, probably last night after dinner. And then he'd switched the doorknobs on the closet, moved the boxes into the closet, and locked the door.

This wasn't a lock on a backyard shed, out in the open where thieves might prowl. This was a lock on a closet inside the house.

This lock was there to keep Mom and me out. Or maybe just me?

What was Bran so desperate to hide?

10

I went over to Mrs. Stuldy's house and had another fat slice of her coffee cake. And then I ran errands for the people she'd recommended. It was the hottest part of day and I was crazy not to be holed up in air-conditioning. But I welcomed the sweat running down my face and streaming into my eyes. I welcomed the blisters forming on my heels, the sore muscles in my legs. It was like I thought the sweat could wash away all my confusing memories of Bran acting weird. It was like I thought my aches and pains could distract me from how I'd felt staring at that locked door.

But I couldn't escape the mystery of Bran.

At Eckerd's, where I stopped for Advil for Mrs. Mathers, they had a huge pile of sale circulars right by the front door. I picked one up and read it, cover to cover. And then I read it again, just to make sure I hadn't missed anything.

They didn't have Energizer batteries on sale. They didn't have any batteries on sale.

"Is this the circular for this week?" I asked the girl behind the counter.

"Sure," she said. "Why else would we have it there?"

I wanted to tell the girl, "If you see Bran come in—a tall sixteen-year-old with dark, kind of wavy hair—watch what he buys, okay? And then let me know. You can do that, can't you?"

But the girl had already turned away from me to restock the chewing gum. And she was a stranger. Why would she help me? Why would I confide in her?

I wanted desperately to talk to someone. But the person I always talked to when I had problems was Bran.

What about my friend Wendy back in Pennsylvania? She seemed too far away, suddenly, like she'd been part of a different life. And she'd only known the perfect Bran. She wouldn't believe anything I told her.

Mrs. Study? I'd only just met her, but she seemed the kind of person you could tell stuff to. Except I didn't want her thinking Bran was weird or lying or in trouble. Or that there was something wrong with my family.

I bet her grandchildren were all little angels.

I decided I had to talk to Mom.

Maybe it seems strange that it took me so long to think of her. But for as long as I could remember, Bran had told me— trained me, really—to protect Mom from any problems. When we were little and still went to a baby-sitter, we had one for a while who used to slap our faces when she got mad.

"Don't tell Mom," Bran had whispered to me, day after day. "Mom can't afford to send us to someone better than Mrs. Ellis. Just be really, really good."

And that worked for Bran, because he could sit still when Mrs. Ellis wanted him to, and he always remembered to say *please* and *thank you,* and to not drop crumbs on her carpet. But I was always leaving sticky jelly-covered handprints on her wall. I forgot to pick up my toys. I spilled my glass of milk all over the kitchen floor. I got slapped a lot.

But neither of us ever told Mom about Mrs. Ellis, even after she moved away and we got a new baby-sitter.

Talking to Mom now would be like breaking all the rules of our family. But I knew I had to do it.

11

My plans were stymied right away. Mom
stayed at the university until midnight the next few nights—I
only spoke to her by phone when she called to say not to wait
for her to eat dinner. I couldn't exactly say, "Explain Bran to
me," over the phone, especially when I could hear people
behind her calling out, "You done with that phone yet?" So I
waited and kept watching Bran.

But he was away a lot too. The Shrimp Shack put him on
double shifts for a while because they were short staffed. Some
nights he barely beat Mom home. I was glad to have my errand
route to distract me.

I was glad for Mrs. Stuldy, too. I got in the habit of finishing
at her house, whether she'd had me run any errands for her or
not. I barely saw Mr. Stuldy—he was a quiet type, who always
seemed to be on his way out the door just as I was coming in.
He'd nod politely and say, "Oh, Early's in there waiting for you.
Go on with you." He was so unnoticeable, it was several days
before I thought to wonder why Mrs. Stuldy was having me
run her errands, instead of asking her husband to do them.
But by the time I started wondering, I had it all figured out.
Mrs. Stuldy needed company.

Every day when I got there, she always had something
home baked waiting on the kitchen table: apple pie, chocolate

chip cookies, hazelnut cake. And the dessert was always gone and replaced by something new the next day. By Friday I felt like I'd known her long enough to ask where all the extra baked goods went.

"Oh, Mr. Stuldy takes them down to the senior center with him every morning," she said. "They like my cooking down there."

"Why don't you go with him?" I asked. I'd been past the senior center on my errands. It was a huge building with more windows than walls, so I could see the dozens of old people in there sitting around talking and laughing, playing cards or checkers or chess, doing the funny stretching exercises that old people do. Once I saw a whole row of women painting faces on china dolls. Mrs. Stuldy seemed like the type who would like painting dolls. She seemed like the type who'd want to be laughing and talking in there with the best of them.

Then I remembered that she couldn't walk very well.

"I'm sorry!" I said. "I shouldn't have asked that. It's probably too hard for you to get there, isn't it?"

"No," Mrs. Stuldy said, with a heavy sigh. "They'd send the van for me, if I wanted. I just don't fit in real well down there."

"You don't?"

She sighed again.

"Some of the women have said some things about my son— I just don't feel I can sit next to them and tat and crochet like it's no big deal."

"What about your son?" I asked, bewildered. Why was it that suddenly everyone around me was filled with secrets?

Mrs. Stuldy looked straight at me.

"He's in prison," she said in an unwavering voice. "That's

why I have all his furniture. We're waiting until he gets parole—if he gets parole."

I couldn't believe it. Someone related to wonderful Mrs. Stuldy was in prison?

"What did he do?" I asked, before I realized what a rude question it was.

Mrs. Stuldy answered me anyway.

"He got in with a bad crowd, and they decided to rob a bank. Sam was the one with the gun. He says he didn't mean to shoot anyone, just scare them. . . . ," her voice trailed off. "He's down at Stillwater. I go see him every month. I think—I think he's sorry now. He's repented, and if they let him out, he'd try harder not to get in trouble again. He's apologized to the family of the man he killed. But I don't reckon that brings him back to life."

I didn't know what to say.

"I was so mad at Sam when it happened," Mrs. Stuldy said. She wasn't looking at me. It was almost like she was talking to herself. "Here I was calling myself a Christian, and going to church every Sunday, and singing songs about forgiveness, and I couldn't forgive my own son."

"Well, if he killed somebody—," I said. And then I wanted to take my words back, because Mrs. Stuldy looked like I'd punched her.

"He did," Mrs. Stuldy said. "No matter what else he does with the rest of his life, he'll always have to carry that around, that he ended another man's life."

The way Mrs. Stuldy spoke, it seemed like each word coming out of her mouth weighed too much, like stones she could barely lift. That made me think that maybe the reason she walked with such difficulty wasn't bad hips or old age, but the burden she carried.

"I see why you can't forgive him," I said in a small voice.

Mrs. Stuldy sighed.

"Oh, but I *should*," she said. "I'm trying to. I'm trying real hard. I pray about it all the time. And sometimes I think I could forgive him for taking that man's life. But . . ." She glanced around and lowered her voice, even though there was no one in the house but her and me. "Do you want to know what an awful person I am? Sometimes I think I would have forgiven Sam years ago for the murder if it weren't for what it did to me. I didn't know the dead man from Adam. I could forget about him. But I have to listen to the other so-called ladies whisper about me while they're bragging about their own children. I probably won't ever have grandchildren because of Sam being in prison. Because he's my only child. I can't sit here thinking back on all my happy memories of him as a little boy without thinking, 'And then he grew up and killed a man.' Don't you see how selfish I am?"

Mrs. Stuldy blinked, and there were tiny droplets of tears caught in her eyelashes.

"You're not selfish," I said loyally. I didn't know what else to say. I'd never had a conversation like this before in my life. I was kind of proud that Mrs. Stuldy trusted me with her story. But it was awful, too. It scared me. What if something like having a criminal in the family was contagious? I was worried enough about Bran as it was.

Then I remembered how I'd assumed that Mrs. Stuldy had at least a dozen grandchildren to spoil, and they were all little angels. I remembered how I'd seen her the first time I'd met her, as just some old lady in a gaudy dress. Uncomplicated. Good at baking cookies.

"I'm sorry about Sam," I said. "I'm real sorry."

Mrs. Stuldy was wiping her eyes. Suddenly something else struck me about her story.

"Wait a minute," I said. "Did you say you go visit him in prison? Even though you're mad at him?"

"Of course," Mrs. Stuldy said. "He's my son."

I tried to imagine Mrs. Stuldy walking into one of the prisons I'd seen on TV—some place with concrete and razor wire and grim-faced guards. She would look as out of place as a gardenia.

"What do you talk about?" I asked.

"Memories," Mrs. Stuldy said, looking wistful. "And what he's going to do when he gets out of prison. All the *good* things he's going to do. It's—it's the best part of my month, going to visit Sam."

And for a minute she almost looked happy again.

"You still love him," I said, amazed.

"Of course," Mrs. Stuldy said.

That wasn't how things worked in my experience.

"Wow," I said. "I think, I think you really have forgiven him. Because—" I hesitated. Bran had said I wasn't supposed to talk about our family. But he wasn't there, he hadn't heard what Mrs. Stuldy had just told me. And I wasn't going to talk about what was happening in my family *now*. I just wanted to hear what she thought of things that had happened in my family years ago. My family's history.

"Your son killed somebody and you still go see him every month," I said. "My mom, all she did was elope with my dad and her parents disowned her. They acted like she was dead. They wouldn't even speak to her when they ran into her on the street."

I don't know why, but I started crying then.

Mrs. Stuldy patted my hand across the table.

"There, there," she said.

I sniffled and wiped my nose with the back of my hand. Mrs. Stuldy gave me a Kleenex.

"I've never met them," I said. "I've never even seen a picture of them. Mom won't even speak their names, they hurt her so bad. She says there's no point in having any part of them in our lives. But sometimes—sometimes I think Mom thinks they were right to disown her, because Dad wasn't a good person for her to marry."

I wasn't crying anymore, but Mrs. Stuldy kept patting my hand.

"There's no excuse for disowning a child," she said sternly. "Oh, it's awful what people do to each other."

"Mom says she doesn't think they ever loved her," I said.

"Now, that's just plain wrong," Mrs. Stuldy said. "Everyone should have parents who love them."

Hearing Mrs. Stuldy say that made something shift in the way I thought about my family. I remembered when I was really little, thinking my parents' story was like a fairy tale. My grandparents were like the evil stepmother in *Cinderella*, like the witch in *Rapunzel*—just obstacles to true love. Even though my dad had moved out when I was just a baby—moved clear out to California, about as far away as he could go—I still believed they would get back together. Then I saw Dad that one time when he and his parents came to visit, and even at five, I saw that he and Mom were all wrong for each other. He had a motorcycle and wanted to take Bran and me on it. Mom said, "You've got to be kidding. They're not even allowed to ride a bike without a helmet, let alone a motorcycle. And you've had too much to drink." And then they fought, and Dad's parents took his side, and pretty soon Dad and his parents went away. And I was happy. I liked our family being just Mom and Bran and me.

But sitting there with Mrs. Stuldy, I saw how sad it was for Mom not to have parents who loved her no matter what. I saw how sad it was for her to be alone.

Mrs. Stuldy's wrinkled old hand stayed on top of mine.

"I'm sure you and your brother are great comforts to your mother. I'm sure she's proud of you. You're a good child," she said.

"Bran is too," I said loyally.

"Yes," Mrs. Stuldy said as she poured herself another cup of tea. "I'm sure he is. He seemed a little troubled that day he was here."

So even Mrs. Stuldy had noticed. I wasn't used to people calling Bran *troubled*. Usually they raved about what a wonderful teenager he was, how responsibly he behaved, what a bright future he had ahead of him.

"He's under a lot of pressure." I made excuses for him. "He's supporting us while Mom goes to school full-time."

Too late, I remembered Bran telling me not to talk about what he and Mom were doing. But this was just with Mrs. Stuldy, not the other neighbors. And it was in Bran's own defense.

"Bran's really eager to have Mom succeed, because he's the

one who talked her into moving to Florida in the first place," I said.

I remembered all our dinner discussions last winter, the snow blowing in through the cracks around our front door. It was Mom's friend Carlene who started talking about Florida.

"Why are you in this flea-bitten town anyway?" she'd asked Mom. "Just because your man left you behind when he dropped out of college . . . Let's go south! Let's lie on the beach! Live a little, Becky!"

"I'm trying to finish college," Mom had said quietly. "That's why I haven't left yet."

And Bran had chimed in, "I just saw something on the Internet the other day at school—there's a university in Florida that has a special program for single mothers."

From then on, the Florida talk was hot and heavy in our apartment, even as it got colder and colder outside. We barely got anything for Christmas, we were trying so hard to save our money to move. Carlene was going to come with us and chip in part of the gas money and rent. And then—suddenly it was February and we were leaving Pennsylvania, just Mom and Bran and me. I don't know why Carlene didn't come. I just remember waking up in the middle of the night, when we'd been driving straight through. We were parked at some rest stop in Georgia or Tennessee—some state between Pennsylvania and Florida—and Mom was crying.

"What am I doing?" she moaned.

And Bran had answered quietly, "You're moving your family to another state, where there's more opportunity. People do it all the time."

"No," Mom said bitterly. "I got carried away by someone

else's fantasy again. And then, even when it didn't work out with the other person, I just forged ahead. Why don't I stop and think? Why don't I quit for once?"

"Mom," Bran said patiently. "You're going to wake Britt."

And then they talked in hushed voices in the front seat while I was curled up in the back. I wasn't worried about Mom crying. I wasn't worried about whether or not it was a good idea to move to Florida. I knew Bran could take care of everything. The murmuring I heard from the front seat was soothing, like a lullaby. I fell back asleep feeling safe and cozy. And in the morning, when I woke up for good, everyone was cheerful and the Florida sunshine was streaming in the windows.

"Looks like your brother just got home," Mrs. Stuldy said now, bringing me back to the present.

She had taken our dishes over to the sink and was leaning on the counter looking out. I went and stood beside her. Bran was pushing his bicycle alongside the Marquises' house. I was going to rap on the window and wave, but something stopped me. Bran bent down just then, peering at something near the ground. His dark hair fell across his forehead, and he looked from side to side before rubbing a finger on some steel-and-glass contraption attached to the house. Without trying to, I remembered one of those stupid vocabulary words that Ms. Rogers, my English teacher back in Pennsylvania, had worked so hard to get us to learn: furtive. Bran was acting furtive.

I wished Ms. Rogers had never taught me a word like that. It made Bran seem guiltier than ever.

"Something wrong with your electric meter?" Mrs. Stuldy asked.

"Huh?" It took me a minute to understand what she meant.

The thing Bran was looking at was an electric meter. "I don't think so," I said. "He's just—making sure everything's all right. That's how Bran is."

But the way he crouched over the meter, glancing from side to side once more, he didn't look like someone making sure everything was all right. He looked guilty. About an electric meter? Why? I thought about the way Bran had acted about the air-conditioning, and how even now he always seemed to be inching the thermostat upward, when Mom wasn't looking, so the air almost never kicked on. And now that I thought about it, Bran had had an odd look on his face the second night the timer light clicked on, and he announced, "Oh, the Marquises want us to leave the timer alone. Just in case." Lights and air-conditioning and the electric meter . . . There was a clue in there somewhere. But I didn't understand what it was a clue *to.*

I knew Bran wouldn't be involved in anything like a bank robbery or murder. But Mrs. Stuldy's story made me even more worried.

I looked over at Mrs. Stuldy, and she looked almost as puzzled as I felt.

"Bran is so careful about things like that—things most kids wouldn't even think about," I said quickly, trying to convince myself as much as her. "Boy, when the Marquises hired him to house-sit for them, they really got the right person."

My voice was too loud and cheery-sounding. I'd never heard myself sound so fake. But Mrs. Stuldy just nodded and said, "Reckon so."

I was walking home from Mrs. Stuldy's

just as the mailman came up our front walkway.

"Here," he said, handing me a thin stack of papers. "You can save me a few extra steps."

He was sweating like crazy in his blue uniform—I couldn't blame him for wanting to walk a little less.

I let myself into the house and glanced at the mail. It was all junk and ads, nothing interesting. I started to drop the whole pile onto the coffee table. Then I remembered how Bran had acted about the Eckerd's sale circular just a few days earlier. I started looking at the ads carefully. Carpet cleaning, pizza coupons, offers to order vitamins through the mail . . . All addressed to occupant or current resident, except for one furniture-store ad that was labeled JOHN MARCUS.

Marcus, not Marquis.

Alarm bells started going off in my brain. Everything else was right in the address—852 Sundial Lane, Gulfstone, Florida. Even the nine-digit zip code. But I stared at the name, the *cu* that was supposed to be a *qui*. I stared until the letters blurred before my eyes.

What if the Eckerd's circular had also said Marcus, instead of Marquis? What if that was the reason Bran had ripped the front page off the ad and hidden it in his pocket?

But why? Why did it matter?

I thought again about how Bran had been so careful writing down the Marquises' name. That seemed weirder than ever.

Bran came in through the back door just then.

"Hey, Bran, look," I said, holding the furniture ad out toward him. "I think you must be wrong about how the Marquises spell their name."

Bran glanced down at the ad as if it were a piece of roadkill that had been rotting in the Florida sun for days. But when he spoke his voice was carefully casual.

"Hunh," he said. "That's just a mistake. Companies misspell people's names all the time. I bet we'll see lots of mail with the wrong name on it this summer."

But he took the ad and the rest of the mail from me. He tossed it in the trash can.

"Shouldn't they, you know, forward the Marquises' mail to them in New York?" I said. "So we don't get their letters?"

"They only do that with first-class mail," Bran said. "Not ads."

His voice sounded so strange—so glum—I looked at him quickly. He smiled back at me—not a "Gosh, isn't this a great day, aren't you a great sister" smile, but a "Who? Me? I'm not hiding anything" smile.

I might not have been used to Bran hiding things, but I was his sister. I could see past smiles like that.

"Mrs. Stuldy and I were wondering what you were doing outside, with the electric meter," I said.

"The electric meter?" Bran said. "Nothing. Just looking."

I stared at him doubtfully.

"Look, I've got to go mow," Bran said. "Would you just stop

acting so . . . suspicious about everything?"

And then, even though it was about 70 billion degrees outside, he stalked out the door.

I watched though the kitchen window as he unlocked the shed, then crammed the key back into his shorts. I thought about sneaking into the shed while his back was turned, but the backyard was too small. He'd see me for sure.

I'd have to pin all my hopes on Mom.

It was only later—after I'd watched some TV, after Bran had finished mowing, after I'd dragged a couple loads of our clothes to the Laundromat and back—that it occurred to me to fish the furniture ad out of the garbage can to show Mom. I wanted all the evidence I could get.

I pulled an apple core, a banana peel and—ugh—a used Kleenex out of the trash. The furniture ad and the rest of the mail appeared to have vanished into thin air. Or—no, there were tiny shreds of paper at the bottom of the trash bag.

Bran had torn the mail into bits. At some point after he mowed, he'd taken the ads out of the trash can just so he could tear them up.

I picked the pieces out of the trash, studied each shred carefully. There were plenty of partial words: *Occupa*—, *Biggest sale of the sea*—, *Sundia*—.

But the tiny square that should have said *Marcus* was missing.

13

Mom did come home for dinner that night, breezing in just as Bran and I were heating up fried clams and French fries left over from the Shrimp Shack. I was getting a little sick of seafood, and reheated French fries are pretty disgusting. But I ate dinner that night without tasting any of it. In my mind I kept rehearsing what I wanted to say to Mom. I just didn't want to talk in front of Bran, because he'd change the subject or make me seem like a silly, snoopy little kid.

He kept looking over at me anyhow, watching me while I watched him.

No wonder we left it to Mom to do most of the talking.

"Would you believe I have my first set of exams next week?" she asked. She gathered her hair away from her face, holding it tight at the back of her head. Then she let it fall back down, as if she were too exhausted even to lift hair. "The counselors warned me that taking such a heavy load for summer school would be intense, but I didn't think it'd be this bad."

"You'll do fine," Bran said comfortingly. "And you can study all weekend. Britt and I will give you total silence."

He shot me a warning look, as if to say, "Don't talk to her about *anything.*"

I'm not sure what kind of look I gave back to him, but I

wanted so badly for Mom to say, "No, no, I don't need that. I want to hear what's on your minds. I've missed you. Tell me everything that's happened the past few days while I was gone." And then I could spill out all my worries and suspicions, even with Bran listening.

Instead Mom just said, "Thanks. You guys are the best."

After dinner Mom spread out her books and papers on the table once again.

"Hey, Britt," Bran said. "I'm going to walk over to the library to use their computers. Why don't you come with me and give Mom some peace?" He was motioning toward the door with his head, as if that were enough to make me go with him. As if I were a puppet that he could control.

Normally he could have.

But when would I get another chance to talk to Mom alone?

"No, thanks," I told Bran.

"No, really," Bran said. "You don't want to disturb Mom."

"I won't 'disturb' her," I said. "I just want to stay home."

"But— ," Bran said.

"It's okay," Mom said, looking up from her books. "If Britt's at least in the same house with me, I won't feel like such a neglectful mother."

Bran looked from Mom to me in desperation. Mom didn't see his expression because she was already staring down at her books again. But I did. He looked frantic. Devastated. Appalled. All those other vocabulary words Ms. Rogers had taught me back in Pennsylvania that I never thought I'd need.

"Well, all right," Bran said weakly. "But, honestly, Britt, if you bother Mom in any way . . ."

He let his words trail off, which made them seem even more threatening.

I wished Mom would say, "Now, Bran, who's the parent here? Since when are you in charge of Brittany?" But Mom would never say that, because Bran had always been in charge of me. Ever since Dad left when Bran was only four years old, Bran had acted like he was my father.

It had just never bothered me before.

Bran slipped out the back door with one last, desperate warning look directed my way.

And then Mom and I were alone.

Mom turned a page, and I sat down on the couch. I'd give her fifteen minutes, I decided. Then I'd ask her to take a study break and I'd tell her everything. I couldn't wait any more than fifteen minutes, because Bran might come back quickly. But I couldn't talk to her right away because she'd just started studying.

The digital clock on the VCR seemed frozen at 7:49. After an eternity, it changed to 7:50. And I was supposed to wait fourteen more minutes?

"Brittany, would you stop that!" Mom snapped.

"Stop what?" I asked. Then I realized I'd been nervously tapping my foot. "Oh, sorry," I said.

I got up and walked over to the table. I'd already interrupted her, so I might as well plunge in.

"Can I talk to you for a minute?" I asked.

"Weren't we just talking at dinner?" she asked. She didn't look up from a diagram of a skeleton she was studying.

"Well, this is something else," I said.

"What?" Mom said impatiently. She looked up. *"What?"*

And then with her frowning at me, I chickened out.

"Why do you want to be a doctor so bad?" I blurted out, because it was all related. If Mom hadn't wanted to be a doctor, we wouldn't have moved to Florida, we wouldn't have moved into the Marquises' house, and Bran wouldn't be acting so weird. Would he?

"Didn't you read my college admissions essay?" Mom asked.

"No, you just had Bran proofread it for you," I said.

Mom sighed.

"Well, I like all the science. I think it's interesting how the human body works. And I want to help people."

"And?" I said, because she didn't seem to be done.

"Well, those are the good reasons, the ones I stressed on my admissions essay. But . . . I can't say I don't think about the money, too. Can you imagine being able to walk into McDonald's and not have to worry that we don't have enough money for a Big Mac? Or thinking that if we buy a Big Mac, we won't be able to afford something else?" She sounded wistful.

"You always say you don't like Big Macs," I pointed out.

"Chicken nuggets are cheaper," Mom said.

This was interesting, though it didn't tell me anything about Bran.

"Doctors aren't the only ones who make lots of money," I said. I'd heard Mom's friend Carlene back in Pennsylvania make that point lots of times. "There wouldn't be enough money in the whole world to pay me to go to school for an extra seven years," she always said. Of course, Carlene also bragged about dropping out of high school.

"It's not just the money. People *respect* doctors," Mom said. "Nobody respects waitresses whose husbands leave them. Nobody respects single mothers."

I should have said, "*I* respect you, Mom. Bran respects you." But Mom was looking at her book again. It was like she'd already forgotten I was there.

"Mom," I said, and took a deep breath. "Don't you think there's something wrong with Bran? Don't you think he's been acting weird ever since we moved into the Marquises' house?"

"No," she said without looking back up. She began checking off the names of bones on a chart.

"But—," I said.

"Look, Brittany, I'd love to have a nice long chat with you, but I really don't have time for this," Mom said.

"But it's important!" I wailed. "Bran's been acting sneaky! He was sneaking around this afternoon looking at the electric meter! He—" I wanted to tell her about the missing name from the furniture ad, but I didn't want to admit I'd been picking through the trash, not with her looking so doubtfully at me. I searched for my strongest argument. "He waited until you and I were both supposed to be asleep Monday night before he moved the boxes out of the storage shed. He's hiding something! He even put a lock on his closet!"

Mom started laughing.

"Really? A lock? Bran?" she said.

"Yes," I said, practically pouting. I hadn't expected Mom to laugh. "You should make him open the closet and show you everything that's inside there."

I felt like I'd thrown down a challenge. Finally I'd managed to say something right. Finally Mom would be able to help me solve this.

But Mom was shaking her head grimly.

"No," Mom said. "That's exactly the kind of thing my parents would have done."

"But what if he's got—I don't know—drugs in there? What if he's hiding evidence for the Marquises or something?" I couldn't exactly see Mr. and Mrs. Marquis as a pair of drug dealers, but I had to get Mom to see how serious this was.

Mom kept shaking her head.

"Brittany, it's—Bran's a teenager. I'm surprised he's waited this long to start wanting some privacy. Maybe he's got a picture in his closet of some girl he thinks is really cute, but he's too shy to ask out. Maybe he's got acne medicine in there and he doesn't want us to know he's using it. Maybe . . . I don't know. There are dozens of perfectly legitimate reasons he might want to keep you and me out of his closet."

"But if you made him show you, you'd know for sure—"

"Look," Mom said, putting down her pencil. "I'll tell you a little story I've never told anyone. When I was fifteen my parents stole my diary from beneath my mattress, where I'd hidden it. They read it out loud, to each other, right in front of me. They criticized everything I'd written, told me how stupid I was, then threw the diary away. And when they got done, I felt horrible. I cried for days. And they criticized me for that, too. *That's* why I would never force Bran to show me what's in his closet. Because I don't want to humiliate him. And I trust him."

Mom reached for one of her other books to study.

"Maybe they were right to do that," I said sulkily. "You were probably just writing about how much you wanted to run away with Dad."

Mom froze, her arm still outstretched.

"Actually," she said icily, "what I wrote in my diary was how much I wanted to be a doctor. And they did everything they could to kill that dream. That was one of the reasons I *did* run off with your father, because I didn't think I had any better choices."

Mom picked up her textbook and clutched it like it was all she had. She looked like it hurt just to say the words *my parents* and *your father.* If I'd wanted to win Mom over to my point of view, I'd done everything wrong. There was such a chill between us now, we wouldn't need air-conditioning the rest of the summer.

I kept talking anyway.

"But—it's like I said before, Bran was moving boxes out of the shed after midnight Monday. Why would he do that?"

"Maybe that was the only time he had," Mom muttered distractedly. "He's working full-time, you know."

She picked her pencil up again. I saw her check off *tibia* and *femur* on her list of bones.

"And—" I felt like I was grasping at straws. "On Tuesday he didn't want me to be seen out on the front porch because he said the Marquises thought that made a house look 'trashy.' Isn't that crazy?"

"It's not his fault if the Marquises have some bizarre ideas," Mom said, still staring at her bone chart. "They probably asked him to check the electric meter, too."

"But—"

Mom pressed her pencil down so hard the lead point broke.

"Brittany, that's enough!" she snapped. "This is driving me crazy. Bran has done nothing wrong! You're just bored and you're imagining things, and I've got three tests next week and I'm not going to be ready for any of them if you don't leave me alone!"

"Okay, fine! I'll leave!" I huffed. I stalked out the front door and let it slam behind me.

I wanted Mom to come after me, to apologize, but she didn't. I stood there on the front porch, breathing hard and looking out on a beautiful scene of palm trees and tropical flowers and the tidy houses across the street. And I hated them all. The beauty seemed fake. At least back at Sunset Terrace, with its ugly mold and overflowing Dumpsters and broken doors, Mom and Bran and I had been united, a team—the three of us against the whole rest of the world. Now Bran was acting strange and secretive and guilty, and Mom was mad at me. And I was all alone.

"Hi, Britt," someone said.

I looked around—it was Mrs. Stuldy. She and Mr. Stuldy were sitting out on their porch, enjoying the cool evening. (*See?* I wanted to say to Bran, to Mom, to the Marquises. They *don't think it's trashy to sit on their porch.*)

"Hi," I said back.

"Want to join us?" Mrs. Stuldy said. "It's a nice night."

Okay, so maybe Mrs. Stuldy liked me. But I didn't feel like talking just then.

"No, thanks," I said, kind of choking on the words. "I've got to go . . . around back."

I went around to the backyard because it was darker there. I crouched down against the side of the house and I cried a little. I realized I'd never said anything to Mom about the Marcus/Marquis confusion and the missing scrap of paper. But

I didn't think it mattered. I didn't think Mom would have listened to me about that, either.

I knew just how Mom must have felt when her parents threw out her diary and made fun of her dream of being a doctor.

It wasn't fair, because she'd been right to want to be a doctor.

And I was right about Bran.

14

Mom did apologize later, when I finally dried my tears and walked back into the house, blinking in the unfamiliar light. But the apology was all about how she was sorry she was so stressed out and "I know this isn't a very enjoyable summer for you" and "I do appreciate everything you're doing to help—thanks for doing laundry today" and "Why don't you call up some friends and arrange to meet them at the beach or the park or something?"

She didn't seem to remember that I didn't have any friends in Florida. And she didn't say anything about Bran.

It was like she hadn't heard a single word I'd said.

I held back a tide of angry words and just muttered, "That's okay. I think I'll go to bed now."

"Get some sleep for me," Mom said a little wistfully.

And I almost felt sorry for her then, almost turned around and said, *Look, I'm not making all this up. I know studying is important, but don't you want to know that Bran lied about how the Marquises spell their name?* But I wasn't sure that he'd lied, and I was still mad at Mom. I just nodded stiffly and went to my room.

Figuring out Bran was going to be entirely up to me.

For the next few weeks, though, he seemed to be acting almost normal. Nothing else happened. Bran worked, Mom went to school, and I ran errands for all the old people in our neighborhood.

And Bran always got to the mail before I did.

Then one afternoon when I was standing in the hot Laundromat tossing clothes into the washer, I felt a hard lump in the pocket of a pair of Bran's shorts. I'd already dropped a whole pile of clothes in before the sensation registered. But I quickly leaned into the gaping washer and yanked the shorts back out.

They were the threadbare, ragged shorts Bran usually wore when he mowed the yard. Holding my breath, I reached into the pocket. The lump wasn't just a lump. It had sharp points.

I pulled my hand back out, holding a round circle of metal.

A key ring.

A key ring with three keys dangling from it.

I fingered each key in turn, whispering, "House key. Shed key. Closet." I must have looked as loony as some of the old people I occasionally saw shuffling around Gulfstone talking to themselves. I threw the rest of the clothes into the washer, slammed the door, jammed the quarters into the machine to start it. And then, clutching the keys, I sank into one of the plastic chairs across from the washer.

Bran must have put the keys in his pocket when he'd mowed the day before. Then he'd forgotten to take them out when he came into the house and took a shower. And, miraculously, he hadn't even remembered them when he got up and went to work that morning.

I stared at the clothes spinning round and round in the washer, and my thoughts seemed to churn just as violently.

Bran had gone in to work at eleven. He probably wouldn't

be home until four or five—maybe not until eight or nine. And Mom wouldn't be home any sooner than that. I was holding the keys to the shed and Bran's closet. I'd have plenty of time to look at everything in all of the Marquises' boxes.

I did hesitate. I remembered Mom speculating about why Bran might want some privacy. *Maybe he's got a picture in his closet of some girl he thinks is really cute, but he's too shy to ask out. Maybe he's got acne medicine in there and he doesn't want us to know he's using it.*

I wouldn't make fun of him if he was hiding acne medicine in his closet. If everything he was hiding was perfectly innocent, I'd never let on that I'd seen the inside of the shed and his closet.

But if he was hiding something awful . . .

I looked at the keys again, and they seemed to have a sinister gleam to them. I remembered a story that one of our babysitters had told me when I was little, which had given me nightmares for weeks—Blackbeard? Bluebeard? Something like that. It was about a young girl who married a man with a strange-looking beard. And he was perfectly nice and wonderful to her and gave her the keys to every room in his mansion, except he told her she must never, ever open the closet under their stairs. And of course that made her curious, so she opened the closet and found the bodies of all his former wives, whom he'd killed. And then he found out that she'd looked in the closet and he tried to kill her, too.

I knew Bran wasn't hiding dead bodies in his closet.

But that made me even more determined to look in the closet and the shed, to prove to myself that he wasn't doing anything wrong.

The buzzer on the washer went off, and I jumped guiltily. Then I scrambled up and hurriedly dumped all the clothes back into our laundry bag, even though they were all soaking wet.

I didn't have any time to waste waiting around for the dryer. I had a mystery to solve.

15

As soon as I got home I attacked the
shed. I unlocked the door and slipped inside, then pulled the
door shut behind me. This, of course, made the interior of the
shed as dark as night, and I debated: take the risk of leaving the
door hanging wide open, or waste time going into the house for
a flashlight?

In the end the problem was solved for me. As I was groping
around, trying to get my bearings, I found a switch on the wall.
I pressed it, and a light glowed overhead.

"Thank you, Mr. Marquis," I muttered.

Then I settled down to the serious business of searching
boxes.

The odd-looking plastic plates and cups with the plaid pattern filled two of the boxes, and two others held nothing but
ancient-looking cups and glasses. The other boxes I looked
through yielded odds and ends: vases, baskets, knickknacks. I
found the collection of ceramic cats from my room in the last
box, and it made me want to cry. It wouldn't have mattered if I
had. I had so much sweat running down my face that I wouldn't
have even noticed a few tears.

I sat back on my heels and looked at the pile of boxes I'd just
finished searching. Had I missed something? I leaned over the
stack of boxes, but there was nothing behind them.

"Why was Bran so worried about this junk?" I asked out loud.

I thought about what Bran hadn't bothered boxing up, what he'd left sitting out in the Marquises' house: the TV, the VCR, what looked like a brand-new stand mixer.

Bran hadn't hidden away anything valuable. He'd just hidden everything old.

This seemed like a clue, but I didn't know what it meant. I carefully put everything back the way I'd found it and locked the shed again. Then I rushed into the house.

At first Bran's closet was no more revealing. It just confirmed what I'd already thought. I didn't find any acne medicine or other embarrassing teenage-boy secrets. I just found boxes of old games and old books and old blankets, including the quilt he'd taken from my room.

Why had Bran hidden away this falling-apart Monopoly and left a brand-new game of Sorry in the TV stand? Why had he packed up all these musty-smelling *Reader's Digest* condensed books and left the new-looking row of Mary Higgins Clark mysteries on the built-in bookshelf in the sunroom? Why had he stored an afghan so ancient that it was unraveling, but let me sleep on Marquis sheets that were so new they were stiff?

I felt more and more confused the more boxes I opened. I was beginning to give up on solving any mysteries when I opened the second-to-last box at the very back of the closet.

It held pictures. Marquis family pictures.

And suddenly I almost forgot about trying to understand Bran. I slowed down and studied the pictures as greedily as if they were food and I was starving. A pile of loose snapshots was on the very top. They were all of laughing people, all of groups who must have been the Marquises' entire extended family gathered for Christmas dinners and Easter egg hunts and birthday parties. . . . I had barely seen my mother in days and I didn't trust my brother anymore—and, meanwhile, the Marquises seemed to be living their lives in a Hallmark commercial.

I ached a little as I put the snapshots aside and moved on to a stack of framed formal shots.

The very first one was of a dark-haired girl a little younger than me, maybe nine or ten. She had a red ribbon in her hair and wore a red velvet dress. It was one of those Christmas shots people have taken of their kids at JC Penney or Sears or Wal-Mart. (Other people. Mom had never been able to afford it for Bran and me.) This little girl had a trusting, friendly smile. I decided she absolutely had to be a Marquis grandchild.

"What's your life like, little girl?" I asked aloud. She smiled back at me. I decided that Mrs. Marquis had bought the little girl's dress and shipped it from Florida. And Mr. and Mrs. Marquis called Little Girl Marquis's family every week, to find out how she'd done on her spelling tests and how many goals she'd kicked in soccer. And back in their home in New York, the Marquises had pictures all over the place of Little Girl Marquis and—

I remembered I didn't have an eternity to spend staring at Little Girl Marquis.

I dug down a little farther into the box, and there was a framed shot of what I thought must be the entire Marquis family: an old man I recognized as Mr. Marquis, an old woman who had to be his wife, two men and two women who looked to be about my mom's age, and five kids. I almost didn't recognize

Little Girl Marquis because she was only five or six here, but she was wearing another velvet dress—green this time—and she had the same smile. So I was right. She was a grandkid.

I studied the picture intently, trying to figure out which of the grown-ups were the Marquises' sons or daughters and which were in-laws. Then I tried to decide which kids belonged to which grown-ups, and which ones were brothers and sisters and which ones were cousins. Little Girl and two of the boys had dark eyes and dark hair, and the others had light hair and greenish eyes, but I knew better than to jump to any conclusions. Bran's hair was much darker than mine—in fact, he looked more like Little Girl Marquis than like me.

I put the big family photo carefully on the floor and reached down even deeper in the box. I could see the corner of a photo album just below a few more framed photos. I tugged on it, angling it out sideways.

I'd gotten it just far enough out of the box that I could make out three words embossed on the cover, when I heard the sound of a door opening at the back of the house. The door I'd left unlocked in my rush to get to Bran's closet.

"Britt? Hello? Are you here?"

It was Bran.

16

I glanced at my watch quickly, wondering

if I'd just spent five hours staring at the Marquises' family por-
trait. But it was only two o'clock. What was Bran doing home
already?

I heard him coming down the hall toward his room. Quickly
I yanked the closet door shut, hiding inside. I had one foot practically on top of the Marquises' pictures, the other foot
crammed between two boxes, and both hands braced against
the wall. It was a good thing I was small for my age, because I
wouldn't have fit otherwise.

"Britt? Britt?" Bran kept calling. He was in his room now. I
could tell from the sound of his footsteps that he had stopped
near the dresser. I heard a series of rolling noises—he seemed
to be pulling the drawers out of his dresser and then shutting
them, one after the other.

"Where is it?" he muttered, then shouted, "Britt?"

He walked all the way around the room, stopping here and
there, but he didn't come near the closet. As soon as I heard
him leave the room I jumped out of the closet, locked the door
again with shaking hands, then sidled over to the door of his
room.

I peeked out into the hall, but Bran wasn't anywhere in
sight. I stepped out and forced myself to walk casually out

toward the living room, where Bran was still calling for me.

"*There* you are," he said with great relief. "Where have you been?"

"Bathroom," I lied.

"Really? But I just walked past there—"

"Mom's bathroom," I amended. "I like using it sometimes. I like having two bathrooms."

He didn't seem to notice that I was practically panting with relief at not having been caught, that I was still sweat soaked and dirty from being in the shed.

"Oh," he said. "Hey, have you seen my keys? I got to work and I didn't have them, and I'm on my break now so I came home to look for them—I've only got five more minutes—"

Trying to keep my hands from trembling, I pretended to reach into my pocket, then lifted the key ring high into the air. I let the keys dangle before his eyes.

"Oh, thank you," he said. "I was so scared I'd lost them."

"You don't have any copies?" I asked, trying to sound casual.

"Just of the house key. Just the ones you and Mom have," he said. "Of course, the Marquises have extras of the other two, but I don't want to bother them."

I would have bet anything that the Marquises didn't have a copy of the closet key, but I didn't tell Bran that.

"You left them in your shorts," I said. "I found them when I was doing laundry."

Bran looked down, and he seemed to take in the wet laundry I'd basically thrown down on the living-room floor.

"I, uh, ran out of quarters," I lied. "I came home to get more so I can dry everything."

I didn't think my lie sounded any more convincing that any

of the lies Bran had told. But he just reached down into his pocket and came up with a handful of change.

"Here," he said, dumping the coins into my hand. "Use these."

I felt like I was being bribed.

"Hey, thanks again," Bran said. "Now I've got to go. Good luck with the rest of the laundry!"

And then he ran out the door again.

I sank into the couch. Now that the emergency was over, I felt like the bones in my legs had melted and couldn't hold me up anymore. I hadn't been caught. I hadn't managed to put away everything in Bran's closet, and if he looked he'd probably figure out that I'd been snooping. But I wasn't sure that he'd bother looking in there the rest of the summer.

I wished that I hadn't locked the closet again. I wanted to look at the rest of the pictures. And I wanted to double-check the words I'd seen on the photo album, to make sure I'd read them right.

Marcus Family Memories.

Marcus, not Marquis.

I could believe a family's name being misspelled on a furniture ad, on an Eckerd's circular. But on a personalized photo album?

I now had proof that Bran had lied. Absolute proof.

But how could I confront him or Mom with the proof without admitting that I'd been snooping? And why did it matter how the Marquises spelled their name?

17

I ate dinner that night in a total daze.
I kept trying to decide: If Mom or Bran asked, "What's wrong
with you?" would I tell them the truth? Would I confess and
accuse Bran all at once?

But Mom and Bran both looked so tired they probably
wouldn't have noticed if I'd suddenly sprouted green hair.

I went to bed early and dreamed about meeting Little Girl
Marquis—or, Little Girl Marcus, I guess. She was wearing her
red velvet dress and kicking soccer balls to me, but I kept missing them.

"Come on," I said, "I want you to meet my brother."

Suddenly she was her younger self, the one in the green velvet dress. She shook her head violently and sucked on her
thumb. Then she pulled her thumb out long enough to say,
"He's bad. He lies."

"No, no, Bran's good. He's the perfect brother. Well, he used
to be. Come on! He'll be nice to you!" I tugged on Little Girl
Marcus's hand, but she wouldn't budge. She kept shaking her
head.

"Then can I meet your family?" I asked. "Please?"

"Won't share," she said, and went back to sucking her
thumb.

I woke up feeling more confused than ever. The Marcuses'

flowered sheets were tangled around my legs. It was late—past ten o'clock. Mom and Bran were long gone. The entire house seemed to echo with secrets and lies.

I got up and got dressed and escaped to Mrs. Stuldy's.

Her kitchen seemed safe and cozy, with the smell of spices in the air and a plate of oatmeal cookies on the table. And yet she had a secret too, about her son the murderer.

I wanted to ask her if her son had ever lied when he was a teenager, but I couldn't. I couldn't ask if she knew how the Marcuses spelled their name, either. Instead, I blurted out, "What are the Marcuses like?"

"Didn't you meet them?" she asked, pausing over her lemonade.

"Just Mr. Marcus. Just briefly," I said.

I didn't tell her how Bran had interrupted when I'd tried to introduce myself, how he'd hustled me out of sight. I didn't tell her how many pictures I'd seen, or how I kept thinking I was missing something. Something obvious.

Mrs. Stuldy didn't seem concerned.

"Oh," she said. She took a drink of lemonade. "They're good people. Good neighbors."

"Good how?" I asked.

"Oh, nice types. They keep their place tidy, they don't make a big racket all the time. Once when one of our trees blew down, John loaned us his chainsaw and helped us clean up."

"Do you know them very well?" I pressed.

"Well enough," she said. "They keep to themselves a lot. But they—they know about my son, and they don't make comments like some people do. That goes a long way with me."

I was temporarily distracted, feeling glad I hadn't asked

about her son lying. I hoped she didn't think I would make comments about her son.

"They do sound nice," I said. I ate an entire cookie before I asked my next question. "How many kids do the Marcuses have?"

"Two, I think," Mrs. Stuldy said. "A girl and a boy. One lives in—Oregon? Washington? Somewhere out West. The other's in New York, I think, close to where the Marcuses live."

Somehow I knew that meant Little Girl Marcus had her grandparents right there, close by, half the year.

"Do you hear much from them during the summer?"

"Nah. Strange, isn't it? Half the year we see them just about every day, at least to say hi over the fence. Other half the year, it's like they don't exist."

"You could call them," I said. "Just to say, 'How are you doing? What's up?'"

I didn't know what I was pushing for. My heart beat strangely. Mrs. Stuldy was shaking her head.

"Never really got accustomed to making those long-distance calls," she said. "Roy—Mr. Stuldy, you know—he goes through the roof any time there's extra charges on the phone bill. He'll bring the bill to me and say, 'Talk may be cheap, Early, but it ain't free. Come to think of it, it ain't even very cheap.' Then all I hear about for weeks is how we're on a fixed income. Just once I'd like him to tell me who isn't."

I finished my cookies and went to Eckerd's for liniment for Mrs. Stuldy's back. Then it was Winn-Dixie for Mr. Johnson's groceries and a new *National Enquirer* for Mrs. Tibbetts. Then I knocked on all my customers' doors, just to see if any of them needed anything else. I kept moving. I thought if I walked enough I wouldn't have to think about Bran lying, or the reason for his lies.

But finally, in the late afternoon, I had nowhere left to go but home. I let myself in the front door and just stood there, panting. I had so much sweat streaming into my eyes that everything looked like a mirage.

Maybe that had been my problem the day before. Maybe I'd just misread the name on the photo album.

Surely the Marcuses' name was written down some other place in the house. I should have thought of that weeks ago, after I'd seen the furniture ad. I'd just felt too discouraged to look after talking to Mom.

Now, though, I started with the phone book. I was feeling pretty clever until I reached the middle of the book: The listings skipped from Manning to Mathers. The page that should have contained all the MARs was missing.

Somehow that didn't surprise me.

I could have walked to the public library and looked at the phone book there, but I decided to finish searching the house first. I looked in the desk in the sunroom, in the TV stand, in all the kitchen drawers and cupboards. Nothing. The Marquises/Marcuses might as well not have had a last name, for all the evidence I could find of it.

Or Bran had hidden all the evidence.

I started down the hall to Bran's room, but then I retraced my steps and walked into Mom's instead. I was pretty sure Mom's room was where the Marcuses had slept.

Still, I hesitated on the threshold of the room. I'd barely been in there all summer, except to deliver Mom's clean, folded laundry to her. I felt shy suddenly, like I was intruding, though

I couldn't have said whether I was embarrassed about invading Mom's private space or the Marcuses'.

This was the fanciest room, with pink swirly wallpaper and a bedspread that looked like it was covered with pink and blue and orange and green waves. I wondered if Mom felt like she was falling asleep in a very colorful ocean every night.

I looked through the drawers in the dresser, but they held only Mom's possessions. She had a stack of papers on top of the dresser, and I started sorting through them just to make sure they were all hers, not the Marcuses'. The papers seemed to be mostly information about Gulfstone University: an official brochure, a schedule of Mom's classes, a listing of pre-med requirements. I even came across a copy of her application to transfer to Gulfstone, and I pulled it out of the stack, thinking vaguely that I might as well read her essay since I wasn't having any luck otherwise. A slip of paper fell out of the application packet, and I bent down to pick it up. It was a computer printout that said TRANSCRIPT, COMPTON HIGH SCHOOL, COMPTON, OHIO, and under STUDENT'S NAME, it said, MARCUS, REBECCA JANE.

Marcus, Rebecca Jane.

Rebecca Jane Marcus.

Part of me was so stupid that I actually thought, *Oh, that's weird that someone in the Marcus family would be Rebecca Jane, just like Mom.* And, *Wonder how this got shoved in with Mom's papers.*

But the rest of my brain was setting off alarm bells and sending up flares and scrambling to put a bunch of puzzle pieces together.

Mom's maiden name, which I'd never known before, must have been Marcus.

Mr. and Mrs. Marquis, who'd hired Bran to house-sit, were really John and Mary Marcus.

Bran had done everything he could to prevent Mom and me from finding out how the Marcuses really spelled their name.

Strange coincidences? I didn't think so.

Dimly, through the sirens going off in my mind, I heard someone coming in the front door. It wouldn't have mattered who it was—Mom, Bran, the Marcuses making a surprise visit back from up North. I couldn't hide this evidence, couldn't hide my knowledge of it. I was done with secrets. Still holding Mom's high school grades, I walked out of Mom's room, toward the living room.

Bran was shutting the front door against the stifling heat outdoors.

"You can't lie to me anymore," I told Bran. "I know the truth. Mr. and Mrs. Marcus are Mom's parents, aren't they?"

Bran turned around, totally startled. He seemed about to deny it, but then his gaze fell on the paper in my hand. Several emotions danced across his face at once.

"Aren't they?" I said again. I took one more step toward him. I shook Mom's grades in his face.

He slumped against the door, giving up. Giving in.

"Yes," he said softly. "Mr. and Mrs. Marcus are Mom's parents."

18

For a long time I couldn't do anything
but stare at Bran. I still couldn't make all the puzzle pieces fit
together in my mind.

"Why—why didn't you want me to know?" I whimpered.
"Were you and Mom . . . ashamed of me?"

I was working on some strange explanations in my mind.
Like maybe I wasn't really Mom's kid, I'd been switched at birth
or something, and maybe I was the real reason Mom and her
parents had stopped speaking, and that was why Bran hadn't
wanted Mr. Marcus to see me. But he *had* seen me, he knew I
was staying here. . . .

My thoughts were beginning to make about as much sense
as the *National Enquirer.* I just needed to throw in an alien
abduction or two and my customer Mrs. Tibbetts would love
reading all about it.

But Bran was shaking his head.

"No, no, nobody's ashamed of you," he said impatiently.

"Then why . . ."

Bran was biting his lip. He started to speak, stopped, then
finally muttered, "Mom doesn't know either."

"What?" I exploded.

"She doesn't know whose house this is," he said, grimacing.

"She doesn't know who the Marcuses really are. That's why I said they spelled their name M-A-R-Q-U-I-S, and pronounced it a little differently. I didn't dare change it too much, just in case you or Mom talked to the neighbors. But I wanted to . . . to throw Mom off. You could tell—she was kind of surprised. Jolted, when she heard the name. But I'm sure she doesn't suspect."

So that was why Bran had gotten so panicked about the junk mail. That was why he'd ripped the page off the Eckerd's ad and torn the furniture ad to bits. But that didn't explain everything.

"But . . . Mom talked to Mr. Marcus on the phone," I said. I emphasized the last syllable, the *cus*, without even thinking about it. "Didn't she recognize his voice? Didn't he recognize hers?"

Bran sighed.

"That wasn't really Mr. Marcus she talked to," he said. "It was this kid I knew at school, from the drama club, who always got all the old-man parts in all the school plays. I, uh, kind of set him up. I bet him five dollars he couldn't fool my mom into thinking he really was an old man on the phone. I told him what to say. And then he almost blew it, making the old man funny."

I remembered how Mom had said she'd nearly laughed at Mr. Marquis saying, "Eh?" and "What's that?" And I sort of remembered how carefully Bran had arranged the phone call: "Mom, are you available at four o'clock Saturday? No? How about Sunday afternoon? I'll have Mr. Marquis call you. . . ." I'd thought it was just because the Marquises were busy so much. I hadn't known Bran was trying to fool her.

"But—why?" I said. "Why didn't you just tell Mom the truth?"

"Remember how much she hates her parents?" Bran said. "She wouldn't have wanted anything to do with them. And we needed this house. Don't you see how awful Sunset Terrace was? Didn't you hear the gunshots?"

"Yeah, I did," I said vaguely. I was still trying to make sense of everything. I remembered telling Mrs. Stuldy that Mom's parents had never forgiven her for eloping with Dad. But they evidently had. It had just taken eighteen years.

How many years would it take Mom to forgive them?

I wasn't sure I wanted her to forgive them. I thought about the pictures I'd seen in Bran's closet the day before—all those Christmas dinners and Easter egg hunts and birthday celebrations that Bran and Mom and I had missed. Had anyone ever looked around during those gatherings and sighed, *Oh, if only Becky and her kids were here . . . ?* Had they ever wondered what we were eating while they gobbled down their holiday feasts? Had they ever wondered if we had enough presents under our Christmas tree?

They must have, if Mr. and Mrs. Marcus had ended up loaning us their house. But I still didn't understand how that had happened.

"So—did they call you because they knew Mom wouldn't talk to them?" I asked. "Or did you find them? Isn't it weird that we ended up in Florida, in the same town as them? Or—was that the reason you talked Mom into moving here? Because you'd talked to Mr. and Mrs. Marcus?"

Bran didn't wait for me to put everything together. That was a good thing, since I was having trouble thinking clearly.

"They didn't call me," he said cautiously. He still sounded a little strange, but I barely noticed. I almost felt relieved that they hadn't contacted him—that they hadn't picked him as their emissary over me.

"Then how—?" I asked.

"Remember that special computer course I took last fall back in Pennsylvania? The one on Saturdays, at the college?" Bran said.

I nodded. I remembered Bran trekking off to the college while I slept in or watched TV.

"The teacher, Dr. Sprague, had a thing about privacy on the Internet," Bran said. "So he challenged us to find out everything we could about him. You wouldn't believe what's available online. How much his house was worth, what he owed in taxes . . . Even Dr. Sprague was surprised how much we discovered. He was kind of upset, really. But—that got me to thinking. I'd always been curious about the Marcuses."

"So you found them online?" I couldn't help feeling impressed. "How did you even know their name?"

"Well, I was sneaky. I looked at Mom's birth certificate." Bran had the grace to look ashamed. "But it was totally innocent. I just wanted to know . . . things. I knew Mom grew up in Ohio, and I thought it was interesting that her parents moved to New York right after she left. Like, 'Good riddance, we don't care, don't come looking for us,' you know?"

Bran still sounded awfully mad at Mr. and Mrs. Marcus, especially considering they were loaning us a house for the summer.

"And then I found out that they had the house down here," he said. "I started looking up stuff about Gulfstone. And that's when I found out about the single-mothers program at the university. So, yeah, we sort of did move down here because of Mr. and Mrs. Marcus. But I hadn't met them yet."

I tried to remember how Bran had acted last fall. One week in October I'd stayed home from school with the flu, and he'd come home every afternoon and play Monopoly with me. Had he been thinking about Mr. and Mrs. Marcus then? Three days before Thanksgiving, Wendy had developed a big crush on Bran, and she kept bugging me to invite her over so she could talk to him. But Bran had barely noticed her, just saying hi and bye in his usual polite tone. Had he been distracted, wondering if he should tell Mom about Gulfstone?

I didn't think I'd been thinking about anything at all last fall.

I focused on putting the rest of the puzzle pieces together.

"So when we got to Florida," I said, "you came over here and introduced yourself—"

I was thinking Bran must have had a lot of courage. But Bran was shaking his head.

"No. I didn't tell them who I was. Not, uh, right away, I mean. I just showed up and offered to cut their grass, really cheap. I gave a fake name. And then I just watched them, trying to understand . . . to understand how they could have been so awful to Mom."

"Oh," I said.

I suddenly saw how it must have worked. Wonderful, reliable, conscientious Bran had won the Marcuses over. He'd melted their cold hearts. Maybe they'd said, "Young man, you're a real credit to your parents, whoever they are." And then Bran had said, "Well, actually, now that you mention it . . ." And they hadn't been mad. They'd been—I thought of a word that

Mrs. Stuldy used—they'd been repentant. They'd probably begged Bran's forgiveness, asked how they could make up for the past eighteen years. Probably Bran and the Marcuses had worked out the whole house-sitting scheme together. It'd been their elaborate apology.

It all made sense, and suddenly I really wanted Mom to forgive the Marcuses, like they'd forgiven her. I wanted everybody to stop being angry. Mom would say she'd been wrong to elope with Dad; the Marcuses would say they'd been wrong to throw out her diary and tell her she couldn't be a doctor. And then . . . then Mom and Bran and I would be part of the Christmas dinners and Easter egg hunts and birthday celebrations. I wanted that. I wanted grandparents and aunts and uncles and cousins. I wanted everyone to be happy.

"Bran," I said slowly. "I think . . . I think you should tell Mom the truth. Maybe she wouldn't be as upset as you think. It'd be good for her to know that her parents don't hate her anymore."

I remembered how she'd looked telling me about her parents destroying her diary, destroying her dreams. I could tell the memories still hurt, even after all these years. I didn't want Mom hurting like that anymore.

"No," Bran said, shaking his head. "You don't know the Marcuses like I do. You don't know what you're talking about."

"But—"

Bran pushed past me.

"Look, you solved the big mystery," he said harshly. "Now just forget all about it, okay?"

As if I could.

Bewildered, I followed him down the hallway. The way he

was acting, I could tell he was about to rush into his bedroom and slam the door in my face. I'd solved the mystery, but he was still trying to hide. He still wouldn't look me straight in the eye. Why?

"What's wrong with you?" I asked.

Bran whirled around.

"This isn't your problem," he said. "You don't have to worry about anything. So *don't.*"

And then he did walk into his bedroom and shut the door in my face, but he shut it gently, almost regretfully.

I stood there staring at the grain of the wood door. The door keeping me from Bran. The door belonging to the grandparents I'd never known, might never get to know.

"I could tell Mom myself," I whispered.

I started pounding on Bran's door.

"Hey!" I yelled. "What if I told Mom? What if I wrote to the Marcuses, said I know who they are now? Said they could talk to me, not just you?"

Bran opened the door.

"No, no, don't do that," he begged.

"Why not?" I challenged. I was somebody else suddenly—not wimpy Britt Lassiter who did whatever her brother told her, but an investigative reporter, a prosecuting attorney, a person who'd do anything to get to the truth.

"It's complicated," Bran said.

"I don't care," I said. "You have to tell me everything. Or else I'm telling Mom." I crossed my arms for emphasis. I'd summoned up the two most powerful words a younger sister could use: *I'm telling.* I'd almost never had the chance to use them with Bran before. But they worked.

"Okay!" Bran said. He gulped. "You can't tell Mom or contact the Marcuses because . . ." His face contorted; his gaze flickered away.

"Because?" I prompted.

He looked back at me and his eyes locked on mine. I knew that whatever he was about to tell me, it was going to be the truth.

"I never told the Marcuses my real name," he said in a strangled voice. "And I lied about them hiring me to house-sit. They don't even know we're here."

19

If I'd been dumbfounded before, I was far beyond that now. I reeled back against the wall. I probably would have fallen down if it hadn't been there to hold me up.

"They don't know we're here?" I repeated, trying to make the words make sense. All my rosy little dreams about Christmas dinners and Easter egg hunts seemed to cave in on me. My legs buckled and I slid down to the floor.

So I'd been wrong about something else. Even the wall couldn't hold me up.

Bran crouched down beside me. He was acting like a caring brother again.

"See why I didn't want to tell you?" he said. "I knew you'd be . . . upset. But there's nothing to worry about. Everything's under control. Now."

I thought about Bran frantically moving boxes, hiding trinkets, worrying about air-conditioning and timed lights.

"They don't know we're here . . . ," I said again weakly. "But—they're paying you."

"Just for mowing," Bran admitted. "That's all they hired me for."

"But—you're making extra money. Aren't you? You told Mom—"

"Mr. Marcus is paying me a higher rate over the summer.

Since it's so hot. I just told Mom that extra money was for house-sitting."

Bran was so calm admitting he'd lied. I couldn't understand.

"But I heard Mr. Marcus tell you to be careful with the key. Not to lose it," I said. I didn't care now if Bran knew that I'd been eavesdropping.

"The key to the shed," Bran said. "That's all he gave me."

I blinked up at Bran stupidly.

"Then where'd you get the keys to the house?" I asked. "Mom's key and mine and yours . . ."

"The Marcuses always kept a spare key under a rock in the backyard," he said. "I took it and made copies."

It sounded like something a criminal would do. It *was* something a criminal would do.

The walls of the hallway seemed to be closing in on me.

"Bran, this is . . . wrong," I said. "We shouldn't be here."

"Shouldn't we?" he said. He stared down at me, his eyes blazing in the dim hallway. "And should Mr. and Mrs. Marcus have been so nasty to Mom that it made her want to run off with a jerk like Dad? Should they have refused to help out when Dad left and she lost her job and you and I were hungry? Should they be able to live it up in two houses—two!—while we were going into debt just to pay for a lousy place like Sunset Terrace?"

I hadn't known about some of those "shoulds." I ached all over for Mom. But I mumbled, "Two wrongs don't make a right." Neither did three or four.

"Don't you see how unfair it all was?" Bran asked. "Look." He grabbed something from my hand. Amazingly, I'd still been clutching Mom's high school transcript. He held it up before my eyes. "Did you look at Mom's grades? Straight As. Freshman and sophomore year. And then she dropped out. Brilliant Becky Marcus, future MD, turned into a pregnant teenager with a drunk husband. Did you know I was three years old before she managed to get her GED? And then she kept trying, kept scraping together money for college classes, kept studying while her car broke down and her boss hit her in the face and you and I got strep throat and ear infections and made her miss work and miss class. . . . Don't you know how hard Mom's worked all these years? How hard she's tried? Don't you see how this is her only chance?"

He was so fervent his voice cracked. That seemed to break the spell his words had over me.

"She could have waited another year or two to get into the single-mothers program," I muttered.

"They're not sure how much longer they're going to have funding for it," Bran said. "This may be the last year they accept new students."

I hadn't known that. Nobody had told me.

"The day Mom found that out, I came over here to mow," Bran said, and he dropped his voice low, like he was telling more secrets. "I was so mad I could barely look at Mr. Marcus. He told me about them going back North, and he asked if I could mow for them over the summer and I just said, 'Let me think about it.' And then when I was mowing, I happened to knock over the rock where they kept the spare key, and I saw the key lying there in the dirt, and it was like everything was meant to be, you know? I figured it all out right then, the instant I saw the key. They had a house they didn't need, and we couldn't afford our rent and—and they *owed* Mom. They owed her for all those awful years she had, for everything that went wrong in her life that was their fault. They owe her a lot more than a single summer of no rent. But this is enough. This will do."

I swallowed hard.

"Weren't you scared of getting caught?" I asked.

"I wasn't then," Bran said. He sat down on the floor opposite me, settling into a comfortable pose. "I was so sure this was the right thing to do, I wasn't scared of anything. But since then . . . I've had a few close calls. Remember that day you and I came over here, when I thought the Marcuses had left already? I checked to make sure their car was gone, but then Mr. Marcus came out the door. . . . I was scared to death you'd say something about moving into the house, or that he'd recognize you."

"Why would he recognize me? He'd never seen me before in his life," I said, and I ached a little more. It was one thing to have a grandfather I'd never met. It was another thing to have stood right in front of my own, true grandfather and not known it.

"Silly, you look just like Mom," Bran said.

"I do?" This made me think about myself a little differently. Mom was blond and beautiful. I was blond and easily overlooked.

"Of course," Bran said. "In a strange way, that made me madder than ever, that Mr. Marcus didn't recognize you."

"You didn't really give him a chance to see me, you sent me away so fast," I said.

But I was thinking—what if Mr. Marcus had figured out

who I was? What if he'd looked at me and realized how much he missed Mom? What if he'd started crying and hugged me and hugged Bran and begged us to bring Mom to him? What if Bran had given Mr. Marcus a chance?

Bran was shrugging off the whole encounter.

"And then I came back that same afternoon to hide all the things I thought would give away my secret. All the family pictures lying around all over the house, everything with the Marcuses' name on it . . . I did it in bright daylight, as kind of a test. If anyone was watching the house, if anyone was going to notice what happened here, I wanted to know then, before we moved in," he said.

"The Stuldys noticed," I said.

"Yeah, and you saved us on that one," Bran said. "Acting so innocent . . ."

I wanted to remind him that I hadn't been acting. I had been innocent.

"You saved me with the dishes, too," Bran said. "The Marcuses' furniture is so new I hadn't worried about Mom recognizing any of it—I mean, I was here when those couches were delivered. But I hadn't thought about Mom maybe remembering other things, like the plates and glasses, until you started going on and on about them maybe being wedding gifts. And then I had to scramble to put away everything old. Those first few days, I was terrified Mom would find some, I don't know, some button or something else I'd missed, and say, 'Well, look at this! We had one just like it when I was a kid.' And then that would make her figure out everything. . . ."

"She's not here enough to notice anything like buttons," I said.

Bran didn't seem to hear the bitterness in my voice.

"No, she's not," he said cheerfully. "Or to get the mail—that really freaked me out, when I found out the Marcuses' junk mail wouldn't be forwarded."

"You still had to beat me to the mailbox," I said resentfully.

"Yeah," Bran said. "But usually I could count on the mail arriving early, before you woke up, because the mailman doesn't want to be out when it's really hot."

So I would have known the truth sooner if only I'd gotten up earlier in the morning?

"That one day you got the mail before me, I—I guess I panicked," Bran said. "I'm sorry I was so mean to you."

He was staring at me, waiting for me to say, *That's okay. Apology accepted.* But I couldn't. He kept talking.

"The other thing that worried me was the utilities. But I've been monitoring our usage, and it's not too bad. I looked through the Marcuses' old bills, and they do this thing called levelized billing where they pay the same amount every month, regardless of how much electricity or water they actually use. It's supposed to be an average of what they'd expect to use. Then they get money back or pay in a little extra at the end of the year, when it's all totaled up. So even if they do notice something strange, they won't notice until December."

"When we'll be long gone," I said faintly.

"Exactly," Bran said, grinning.

I started shaking my head, as if I could shake off everything he'd told me.

"This is crazy," I said. "I told Mrs. Stuldy my *name*. The neighbors know we're here. What happens in September or October when they say something to the Marcuses about their 'house-sitters'?"

"That's why I was so upset about your errand business," Bran admitted. "I hadn't worried much about the neighbors—you know we've never known our neighbors anywhere else we lived."

It was true. Back in Pennsylvania we'd had college students around us who came and went at odd hours and were too busy partying or studying to notice us. At Sunset Terrace we'd done our best to avoid our neighbors. We'd pulled our pillows over our heads so we didn't have to hear their fights in the middle of the night.

Bran went on.

"That worried me for a long time. But now I think your errand business is a good thing. You can be like . . . an early warning system if something happens that would make us have to leave." I was glad he didn't spell out what that "something" might be. I imagined us scrambling to pack up and leave in the middle of the night, just ahead of the police.

It was an awful image, but Bran didn't look distressed.

"And in the fall," he said, lifting his chin defiantly, "if Mrs. Stuldy mentions us to the Marcuses, as soon as they hear the name Lassiter, they'll know exactly who we are. And then they won't do anything, because it would make them look bad."

He almost sounded like he wanted the Marcuses to find out we'd been here.

I leaned my head back against the wall and closed my eyes for a minute. I wanted to say, *But what if I want to keep my errand business into the fall? What if I want to keep visiting Mrs. Stuldy?* I wouldn't be able to do that now. I'd be too afraid that Mr. or Mrs. Marcus would see me over the fence, would recognize me. And they wouldn't call out, *Oh, you must be*

Becky's daughter! Oh, we're so sorry. Oh, we've missed her so much. . . . They'd peer at me with narrowed eyes, angrier than ever.

I looked up and Bran was smiling at me from the other side of the hall.

"You know, I really didn't want to tell you all this, but now—it's such a relief to get everything off my chest," he said. "It's been so hard keeping this secret alone. Now it's like we're . . . partners. I'm so glad you'll be able to help me."

And his smile was a familiar one now: open, trusting, honest. I knew he wasn't hiding anything from me anymore. He looked like a huge burden had been lifted from his shoulders.

No wonder. I felt like a double-huge burden had slammed down on me.

"Bran, I—," I began weakly. "I still don't think this is right. I think we should tell Mom. I think we should move."

His smile disappeared.

"Haven't you been listening?" he asked. "Where do you think we're going to move to? How would we pay for another place? Mom took out loans to go to school this summer. She'd have to drop out if we couldn't stay here. And she wouldn't get that money back. We'd be worse off than ever." He reached into his pocket and came up with a crumpled twenty-dollar bill that must have been his tips from the day from work. "This would be about all we'd have to keep us from living on the street."

The bill slipped from his fingers and fluttered down to the carpet.

"I made eight dollars today running errands," I said stupidly.

Bran gave a snort of disgust. Then he stared straight at me, his eyes burning into mine.

"Don't you think I hate living here too?" he said. "I think about how Mr. and Mrs. Marcus treated Mom and I want to punch holes in the walls, I want to smash all their dishes, I want to rip their precious pictures to shreds. I didn't know how mad it'd make me, living here. But I can take it. The best revenge is to get Mom through school. And you can't ruin that."

I wanted to back away from all that anger. I wanted to run next door to Mrs. Stuldy's cozy kitchen, where she'd feed me more oatmeal cookies and talk about forgiveness, not revenge. But I couldn't move. I was locked in place by Bran's burning gaze.

"We can't tell Mom," he said. "Or anyone else."

The old Britt, the one who hadn't spent a month and a half being suspicious of Bran, would have started crying and apologizing, wailing, "I won't tell! I won't tell! I promise!" Anything to get Bran to stop staring at me with such fury—as if I deserved some of that fury myself, just for disagreeing.

But living in the Marcuses' house had changed me as much as it'd changed Bran. I stared straight back at him.

"You couldn't stop me," I said. "If I decided to tell, there's not a single thing you could do about it."

His jaw dropped and his head rolled forward, as if he were too stunned to hold it upright. Then he seemed to recover a little.

"You're right," he admitted. "I couldn't stop you. But you won't tell, will you? You wouldn't do that to Mom. Just because you're mad at me for keeping secrets, just because you're mad at her for being away so much . . . that's no reason to ruin everything."

I squinted back at him, suddenly confused. Was he right about my reasons? Was I just looking for revenge too?

"I want some time to think," I muttered. "I won't tell Mom without talking to you first."

That was my concession to the old Britt, the one who was still hiding inside me, urging me to trust Bran completely. I didn't know about loans and utilities the way he did. And I really didn't know what the Marcuses were like. But I could still hear another voice inside my head insisting, *This isn't right. This isn't right. This time Bran is wrong.*

Bran was watching me carefully.

"Okay," he said. "Think about it all summer long, if you want."

He gave me an ironic half-grin that didn't hide any of his disappointment. I suddenly wanted his open, trusting smile back, the one that said, *We're partners, and I'm so relieved that you're with me on this. I hated being alone.*

We were both alone now. Alone with a huge barrier between us, even though we were sitting barely three inches apart.

20

Bran picked up his money and headed out to the living room. I drifted into my room. It was like neither of us could stand the sight of the other just then.

But I couldn't stand the sight of anything else, either. Seeing the Marcuses' walls reminded me that Bran wanted to punch them. The dresser reminded me of the ceramic cats that Bran had taken away from me and hidden. The closet reminded me of the lock on the closet in Bran's room.

I collapsed onto the bed and stared up at the flat, bland ceiling. The ceiling reminded me that the Marcuses had a roof over their heads—they had two roofs, roofs to spare. And Bran and Mom and I would have none at all if I insisted on telling Mom the truth.

I rolled over and buried my face in my pillow. But the flowered pillowcase made me think that probably the Marcuses had bought this bedding with Little Girl Marcus in mind.

How could they love their other grandchildren but not care at all about Bran and me?

I cried then, dripping tears onto the Marcuses' pillows.

I heard Mom come in the front door, and that scared me out of crying. She couldn't see me like this. She'd *know*.

"Where's Brittany?" I heard her ask Bran.

"I think she's taking a nap," he said. "She was acting really tired—let's not wake her up until dinner's ready."

I felt a surge of gratitude. Even though I'd disagreed with him, he was still covering for me, protecting me. Just like always.

Except—who was he really protecting? Me or Mom? Or himself?

I got up and dried my eyes. I forced myself to walk out into the living room.

"Hi, Mom," I said.

She put her arm around my shoulders and gave me a big hug. I wanted to lean into that hug, to keep clinging to her, but I made myself pull back before she did.

"I thought Bran said you were sleeping," she said. She studied my face. "You look a little peaked. You're not getting sick, are you?"

"Naw," I said. "I'm holding off on all illnesses until I can have Dr. Becky Lassiter treat me."

My voice sounded awfully fake to me, but Mom laughed.

"Good," she said. "Because we won't be able to afford any medical care until then!"

Bran shot me a look, like *See? We can't even afford to get sick right now. And you think we're magically going to be able to afford rent?*

Somehow I got through dinner that night. I did it mainly by focusing on the spaghetti on my plate. Our spaghetti, our plates. That dinner had nothing to do with the Marcuses.

But after dinner, when Mom had settled down at the kitchen table to study, the walls started closing in on me again. It seemed like everything the Marcuses owned was trying to talk to me. The heavy wooden table, which I'd admired before, now said, *See me? The Marcuses go for solid and old-fashioned. That's why they hated your father so much.* The dried flower arrangement on the coffee table said, *Mrs. Marcus dusted me every day. She's very exacting. Even with straight As, your mom could never measure up. And neither can you.*

I even imagined I could hear the voice of Little Girl Marcus, calling from the box of pictures in Bran's closet: *My grandparents love me. They'll hate you if they find out you're here.*

But if I told Mom, if we moved out, would there ever be a chance that they'd love us then?

My imaginary Little Girl Marcus wouldn't answer that question.

"Brittany, what's wrong?" Mom asked, looking up from her embryology books with great concern.

Wonderful. I'd wanted to talk to her so badly a few weeks ago, and *now* she was ready to listen. Now that I didn't know what to say.

"Nothing," I lied. "Why?"

"You've sighed five times in the past five minutes. And you're pale as a ghost."

"I'm just bored," I said. "Maybe I'll go for a walk."

Amazing how lies could grow. Every nerve in my body was jangling—I'd never been so unbored in my life. And I'd walked so much already that day that my feet hurt. But I had to get out of the Marcuses' house.

"Want me to go with you?" Bran asked, pushing aside the checkbook he was balancing for Mom.

"No, that's okay," I said.

Normally he would have persisted. Normally I would have wanted him to come with me. But normal had ended this afternoon.

"Make sure you stay where there are streetlights," Bran cautioned. But he didn't stand up to come along. I think he understood that I needed to be alone. Or he was afraid of crossing me now. I didn't like the thought that I might have some power over him—power because I could still decide to tell Mom his secret. Bran was supposed to be the one in control. I wasn't supposed to be keeping his secrets; he was supposed to be keeping mine. Once, back in Pennsylvania, I'd broken a glass on a day when Mom had a tough final, and Bran had carefully swept up all the pieces, hidden the evidence at the bottom of the trash, and biked down to Wal-Mart to get a replacement glass with his own money before Mom got home.

But living in someone else's house without permission wasn't exactly breaking a glass. It was . . . breaking and entering.

The words came to me from some old police show I'd watched once. I wished I'd never heard them. Breaking and entering was a crime—a bad one. It was what thieves did. But we weren't stealing anything. Were we?

I thought of the electricity that powered our lights, the hot water I used every time I took a shower. I thought of the cooled air I was breathing. All that cost money, even if the Marcuses never noticed.

Maybe Bran can pay them back somehow, I told myself. If we stay. He could send them money anonymously. . . .

Could I bargain with Bran—you promise to pay the Marcuses, I won't tell Mom?

I didn't want to bargain. I wanted to tell Mom. I wanted to leave.

No—I wanted the Marcuses to love us and want us here.

I pushed open the front door and stepped outside. It was

such a relief to breathe air that didn't belong to the Marcuses. The breeze lifted the hair off my forehead, and I closed my eyes and leaned into it. But I was still holding on to the porch railing. The Marcuses' porch railing.

"You shouldn't be out on the front porch. . . . It makes a place look trashy," Bran had said to me, back before I knew the truth. But it hadn't been the Marcuses' orders; it'd been Bran's frantic attempt to keep our presence secret.

I stepped off the porch and walked down to the sidewalk, the public sidewalk, which belonged to all of Gulfstone, not just the Marcuses. I walked past the Stuldys' and saw the glow of the TV in their front window. Just passing their house made my heart pound. What if Mrs. Stuldy found out we weren't supposed to be here? What if I accidentally gave away our secret?

I wasn't sure what scared me most: the thought that she might tell the Marcuses, or the fear that she'd hate me then, that she'd think Bran and Mom and I were a bunch of liars and cheats.

We are, I thought. *As long as we live in the Marcuses' house we're lying and cheating. Bran and me, anyway. Mom's innocent as long as she doesn't know.*

I wished suddenly that I'd never solved the mystery, that I'd never found out anything. Then I could have stayed innocent too.

Except—in spite of everything, I kind of liked knowing that the Marcuses were my grandparents. I liked the way they looked in the pictures. Wasn't there still some way to have them love us?

"You don't know what the Marcuses are like," Bran had told me. And they didn't sound like very nice people from what he and Mom had told me. But that was all from years and years and years ago. Maybe they'd changed.

I walked on, lost in some fantasy of Mom and Bran and me magically melded into the pictures I'd pored over, Mr. Marcus showing me how to swing a bat, Mrs. Marcus cutting flowers with Mom. Bran and me holding up Easter egg baskets with the other five grandchildren—our cousins. The three of us sitting under the Christmas tree with everyone else.

I was so distracted that it's a wonder my feet didn't automatically carry me to Eckerd's or Winn-Dixie. But somehow I ended up on the beach. Sand slid into my tennis shoes, so I took them off and went barefoot. The last glow of sunset hung over the water, and a breeze ruffled the palms behind me. I sat down on one of the swings that were scattered along the edge of the beach. They weren't little kids' swings—they were more like porch swings suspended from metal rods. They were meant for old people. But it was still pleasant to dig my toes in the sand and push, gently, to make the swing sway. I could imagine sitting here with my grandparents, Little Girl Marcus pushing behind us.

I'd told Bran that I wanted time to think, but that wasn't really what I was doing. I was just daydreaming. I couldn't see any path from where I was now—living in the Marcuses' house secretly, illegally—to the happy ending I longed for, with smiles and hugs and kisses all around.

I drew my knees up to my chest and let the swing slow down. I stared off into the distance. At the other end of the beach I could see the lights of the senior center. They were having some sort of dance out on the patio, and the old people were holding on to each other, spinning and turning and sliding with amazing agility. I couldn't have said what kind of a dance they were doing—I'd heard of the jitterbug and the Charleston, from decades ago, but I wouldn't have recognized either one of them. Then the music floating across the water changed, and the old people held their partners tighter. They swayed slowly together, each pair as graceful as the palm trees in the breeze.

I wondered if the Marcuses came to dances on the beach when they were living in Florida, and if they held each other close like the people I was watching. From across the beach the dancing was so beautiful I wanted to cry. Some of those couples had probably been together for forty or fifty years. I thought about how lots of the people I ran errands for were always talking about their husbands and wives, even though they were dead. Mr. Johnson had mentioned Erma so much that I said I couldn't wait to meet her. He'd gotten a sad look on his face and said, "Oh, Erma's been in heaven for twenty years now." Was that the kind of marriage Mr. and Mrs. Marcus had—the kind where they would still dance cheek to cheek when they were eighty-two, the kind where whichever one lived longer would keep the other's memory alive for decades?

But how could they love each other so much and not love Mom?

They were right about Dad being wrong for her, I reminded myself. Maybe Mom had never told them about the divorce. Maybe if they knew—

But no, I'd learned from my errand route that old people saw divorce as something shameful, and children with only one parent as horribly deprived. I'd tried to tell Mrs. Stuldy that I didn't miss my father at all, and she hadn't understood.

"Don't you ever long for him?" she'd asked.

"Of course not," I said. "Lots of my friends just live with their moms or just with their dads. My friend Wendy, back in Pennsylvania, her parents didn't even bother getting married in the first place."

I'd wanted to amaze and scandalize Mrs. Stuldy, but she just shook her head sadly.

"Shouldn't be that way," she'd muttered sadly.

And now, sitting on the beach, I remembered something I hadn't thought about in years.

Back when I was five, the last time I saw my father, I'd cried when he left. I could see the cracked green tile of our kitchen floor as I lay there and sobbed. I don't remember what Mom said to comfort me, but I remember Bran, all of nine years old, bending over and whispering in my ear, "It's okay. We don't need him. It's better this way, just you and me and Mom."

And I'd believed him. I'd trusted him. I'd never longed for my father since.

I wanted to trust Bran now, to leave all the decisions up to him once again. I just couldn't.

But if I started making decisions on my own, what was I going to do?

21

"Give me the key to your closet," I said

to Bran the next morning, as soon as Mom left for school.

Bran jumped, so stunned that he actually knocked the spoon out of his bowl of cereal. Milk dribbled across the table.

"Why?" he asked.

"You have the Marcuses' pictures in there," I said. "I want to see them."

Too late, I realized that I was practically confessing to having snooped in his closet before. Or maybe he would think I was just being logical—he'd admitted hiding pictures, and they wouldn't be safe out in the heat of the shed, so naturally they were in his closet.

It didn't matter.

"You can't show them to Mom," he said, and there was a new tone in his voice, a certain helplessness. If he gave me the key, I could show the pictures to Mom. But if he didn't give me the key, I could still tattle, still destroy everything.

"I'm not going to show them to Mom," I said. "Not without talking to you first. I promise."

The words were out of my mouth before I thought about them. It was force of habit—I was used to having to try to make Bran trust me. But I didn't need to say those words now.

I didn't want to show Mom the pictures anyway. I just

wanted to look at them again myself. All of them.

Silently Bran pulled his keys out of his pocket and twisted one key apart from the others.

"Don't lose it," he said. "That really is the only key. I had to buy a new doorknob with a lock, after you told me things could rot in the shed."

So I'd guessed right about that.

"Why did you bother?" I asked. "If you wanted to tear up the pictures anyway, why didn't you just leave everything out in the shed?"

"I wanted you and Mom to think I was taking care of things," Bran said. "I didn't want to lie any more than I had to. And if we did destroy their property, the Marcuses would have good reason to track us down and take us to court or something."

I watched his face. I was searching for some sign that he'd looked through the pictures too, that he imagined loving grandparents the way I did. But his eyes were hard. He didn't really care. He just wanted to avoid getting in trouble.

"Don't you—," I started.

"What?" Bran said.

"Never mind."

I couldn't explain. Not when his expression looked so much like stone.

I tucked the key in my pocket, and as soon as Bran left for work I went into his room and opened the closet. Several pictures were still stacked on the floor where I'd left them. I carefully set them aside for the moment and maneuvered the box with the rest of the pictures out of my way. Then I pulled out the last box in the closet, the one I hadn't had time to look at before. I opened it now.

It contained letters, bills—every scrap of paper the Marcuses owned that spelled their name right. I even found the MAR page from the phone book. It was so like Bran to keep that, to plan to tape it back in at the end of the summer.

I wasn't impressed. I kept thinking, *If I'd opened this box that other time, I wouldn't have gone looking for other evidence. I wouldn't have found Mom's high school grades, wouldn't have discovered her maiden name.* And would I have eventually told her that the Marquises were really Marcuses and blown Bran's secret without even knowing how far it went?

Part of me wished that everything had worked out that way. Then I wouldn't have had to make any huge decisions. I wouldn't have known what weighed in the balance.

I glanced through the box of papers, but I wasn't very thorough. I wasn't trying to solve any mysteries anymore, just make up my mind, and credit card notices weren't going to help me with that.

I did find one more personal letter in the box. It was a notecard that started out:

Dear Mom and Dad,
Alexa keeps asking when Grammy and Pop-Pop are coming home—she's counting down the days on the calendar, but she still thinks anything but "right now" is too long! We all miss you. . . .

It wasn't a long note, but each word felt like a dagger in my heart. I folded it and put it back in its envelope before it could hurt me any more.

Alexa was probably my Little Girl Marcus. How could the

Marcuses be Grammy and Pop-Pop to her but not even know my name?

I shoved the box of letters back against the wall and turned to the box of pictures. These were just as hard to look at, but I couldn't stop. I was like someone gobbling down a whole box of chocolates—still eating long after I'd made myself sick.

Right under the big family photo was a framed shot of Mr. Marcus with three grandchildren on his lap. Little Girl Marcus/Alexa was messing up his white hair and he was grinning at her with his teeth bared, like a monkey. The other girl and the little boy were practically falling off the chair, but you could tell he had a firm grip on them both. He wouldn't let them get hurt. Someone had decided to write a label at the bottom of the picture—it said GOOFY POP-POP.

I stared at that picture for a long time. I think I wanted to find some evidence in it that Mr. Marcus really was mean, that the clowning around was just an act for the camera. I looked at the way the kids were sitting—were they secretly terrified of their grandfather? Were they trying to get away? Were their mouths open because of screams, not laughter?

No. Everyone was having fun.

I put that picture to the side and dug out the Marcus family album I'd noticed the last time. I turned the pages slowly, examining every detail.

Someone—Mrs. Marcus?—was heavily into scrapbooking. All the pages were decorated with cutesy cutouts, like miniature paper hoes and spades on a page about their garden, sand buckets and starfish on the page showing a beach outing. She'd cut the pictures in creative shapes too—ovals, flower petals, hearts.

And everything was labeled.

Besides Alexa, the other grandchildren were Emily, Michael, Josh, and Noah. Evidently they'd all visited the Marcuses in Florida not that long ago, because there was page after page of pictures of picnics on the beach, children playing in the waves, even a trip to Disney World.

And that wasn't their only trip. Traveling seemed to be a big thing for the Marcuses. So many of the photos showed one or both of them posed in front of some beautiful scene. It looked like they'd taken the whole family with them to Vermont one autumn. I felt like I was getting a minute-by-minute replay of that vacation as I looked through dozens of pictures of the entire group in front of beautiful trees, romping in fall leaves, pointing to signs that said YOU ARE IN VERMONT NOW.

I'd never been to New England. Until I moved to Florida, I'd never been anywhere. But looking at that picture made my lungs hurt, just as if I'd breathed too much crisp Vermont air.

The next album I pulled out of the box was even harder to look at. It was old.

The first picture I saw was of a baby lying in a crib. Holding my breath, I pried it out of its plastic sleeve and looked at the back. It said SUSAN, OCTOBER 197— the last part of the date was too blurry to read. It didn't matter, because the baby wasn't Mom. But Mom would have been a little girl in the 1970s. Mr. and Mrs. Marcus hadn't disowned her yet. There might be a picture of her in here.

I looked through the entire album but didn't recognize her anywhere. Doggedly I pulled every photo out of its place and looked at the back. Not all of the pictures were labeled, but none of the ones that were said BECKY. It was all Susan and Mike.

Had the Marcuses gotten rid of every single picture of Mom

when she left? And then rearranged their photo albums to make it look like she had never existed?

I looked at the front of the photo album. Yes, the album did look newer than the pictures it contained. What a lot of trouble to go to, to rearrange all those pictures.

I began to see what Bran meant about the Marcuses being awful people.

But then I looked back at the "Goofy Pop-Pop" picture and I just couldn't understand. How could someone who clowned around with his grandkids be so horrible?

I put all the photo albums and almost all the pictures back in the box. But I carefully removed the "Goofy Pop-Pop" shot from the frame. And after I locked up the closet again, I took the "Goofy Pop-Pop" picture into my room and hid it between my mattress and box spring. I wanted to be able to look at it again.

Someone who could laugh like that, I thought, *wouldn't be too angry if he finds out that Mom and Bran and I are staying in his house.*

But why had he stayed angry with Mom for eighteen years?

All my thoughts seemed to lead in circles. No wonder I couldn't figure out what to do.

That night at dinner my trick from the night before—focusing only on the food, thinking of nothing else—didn't work. I'd seen so many pictures taken in this house I felt like there were ghosts of the entire Marcus family hovering over us. Had Mom felt like she had ghosts with her ever since she left home? Were they always bad?

Before I could stop myself, I blurted out, "Mom, do you have any happy memories of your parents?"

Bran glared at me. Mom looked up in shock from her left-over shrimp scampi.

"What brought that up?"

Bran's glare intensified.

"It's just—I've been around all these old people, and they're always talking about their kids and grandkids, and it got me thinking about my, uh, relatives," I said.

I shot a look at Bran that said, *See, I'm not giving anything away.* He still frowned, then hastily made his face blank when Mom glanced his way.

"I just wondered if there was anything good about your parents," I said, because Mom hadn't answered yet.

"There wasn't," she said flatly.

"Didn't they ever teach you how to ride a bike? Didn't they ever give you a birthday party? Didn't you ever go on picnics together, or fly a kite, or—"

"Brittany, I don't want to talk about it," Mom said. Her voice was shaky now.

I didn't understand. I'd seen so much bike riding and kite flying in the photo albums, so many picnics and parties.

"But—did you have any brothers and sisters who were nice to you even if your parents were mean? Do we have aunts and uncles out there who might—"

"I said I don't want to talk about it!" Mom said. She stood up abruptly. "I'm not very hungry. I'll be in my room studying, if you need me."

She seemed to be making a huge effort to keep her voice steady, to keep from bursting into tears right there in front of Bran and me.

"Now look what you did!" Bran hissed at me as soon as she was gone.

"I didn't mean to upset her!" I protested. "And I wasn't

going to tell her anything. It's just—the Marcuses look like such a happy family in the pictures."

"Pictures can lie," Bran said.

He started clearing dishes off the table, banging the plates together.

"Have you ever seen a picture of Mom from when she was a little girl?" I asked. "There weren't any in the Marcuses' albums."

"That's because—" Bran winced.

"What?" I said.

Bran took the stack of dishes to the kitchen counter, then he turned around to face me.

"Mom told me a story once, about what happened after she ran off with Dad. She got married in blue jeans and a T-shirt— did you know that? It was a spur-of-the-moment kind of thing. And then her parents were mad, and they disowned her—"

"I know that part," I said.

Bran ignored me. He started running water in the sink.

"But all she had were the clothes she left with," he said. "And Dad's parents weren't too happy either, so it's not like they were going to buy her a whole new wardrobe. . . . So she contacted her mom and dad and said, 'Please, just let me come and get my clothes.' And they said, 'Okay, come at four o'clock Saturday. All your things will be out in the yard. Don't come to the door. We don't want to see you.' And when Dad was driving her out there, they started seeing the smoke from miles away. And when they got there, there was a huge bonfire in the front yard. It was everything Mom owned, everything she'd ever owned. They'd set it all on fire. Her clothes and her hair barrettes and her dolls from when she was a little girl . . . And you wonder why you can't find any pictures?"

He crashed the plates into the sink. I was surprised they didn't break.

I backed away from Bran and clutched the counter.

"That's why I don't feel the least bit guilty about living here," Bran said fiercely. "Mom deserves to have *something* good happen, just once in her life."

"What if the Marcuses have changed?" I asked in a small voice. I was thinking of the "Goofy Pop-Pop" picture. I didn't think the man in that picture would burn all his daughter's possessions. "What if they're nice now?"

"Nobody can change that much," Bran said. He scrubbed a plate, rinsed it, and flung it into the dish drainer. "You know, everyone Mom has ever trusted has ended up betraying her. Her parents, Dad, Carlene . . ."

"What did Carlene do to Mom?" I asked in a shaky voice. I didn't care about Carlene. I just wanted to be distracted from the image of Mom's entire childhood going up in smoke. And from being jealous that Mom had told Bran that story, but not me.

Bran gave me a sideways glance.

"Remember how Carlene was going to come to Florida with us? And share expenses? The night before we were going to leave, she met this guy, fell madly in so-called love, and decided to stay in Pennsylvania. And Mom had already put a nonrefundable deposit on an apartment down here, had already rented the trailer. . . ."

"Maybe Carlene really was in love," I argued hopelessly. I hadn't even liked Carlene that much, but something made me want to argue with Bran.

"Yeah, right, it was love," Bran said derisively.

He was working on the forks and knives and spoons now, furiously sliding them back and forth against the cloth. They were going to be the cleanest silverware ever—that is, if he didn't rub them away to nothing.

He slammed the knives into the drainer and turned to face me.

"Britt, I know you want to tell Mom whose house this is. I know you want to ask her all sorts of questions about her childhood. But you *can't*. Don't be somebody else who betrays her."

I looked back at him—Bran, my protector and defender my entire life, my beloved big brother. And it was like I didn't recognize him. He was so angry he might as well have been a total stranger.

"I don't want to hurt anyone," I mumbled.

"Good," Bran said.

And I knew he didn't understand what I meant. My "anyone" was so much broader than his. It included the Marcuses and Mrs. Stuldy, all my customers. The whole world.

His "anyone" was just him and Mom. And maybe, maybe me.

22

I didn't go anywhere for the next few days. I wasn't proud of myself, but it's like I was hiding out, avoiding everyone and everything. I knew my customers probably needed me, but I let the phone ring without answering it. They'd had some way of getting their Metamucil and Alka-Seltzer and *National Enquirers* before I'd moved in, and they'd find some way of getting them after I left. I couldn't face anyone.

Especially not Mrs. Stuldy.

I just had the feeling that if I walked into her sunny kitchen or took one bite of her sumptuous cooking I'd let everything spill out, whether I wanted it to or not. And, really, I kind of did want to tell her everything. I wanted her to know everything so she could tell me what I should do.

So I couldn't let myself see her.

Instead I just absently wandered around inside the Marcuses' house, fingering objects here and there. I still had the key to Bran's closet, but I couldn't stand the thought of looking at any more pictures. I did open it, though, to pull out the box of old books. I was so desperate I even read some of the *Reader's Digest* condensed novels, but they drove me crazy. I kept trying to figure out what the stories left out.

It rained those few days, which fit my mood and probably

made everyone think I was just a fair-weather delivery girl. But on the third morning, the clouds cleared away and a feeble sun peeked out.

And then, not long after Mom and Bran both left for the day, the doorbell rang.

I thought about ignoring it, but whoever was outside started knocking, too, and hollering, "Britt, Britt, are you in there?"

It was Mrs. Stuldy.

I opened the door and there she was in all her glory, with wild hair and a wild dress. I thought about how hard it must have been for her to walk down her stairs, across the sidewalk, and up our steps. She looked so worried I was tempted to tell her I'd been sick—nothing serious, just a cold—so she didn't feel bad that I hadn't been over to see her. But that might upset her, because she hadn't brought me chicken noodle soup, because she hadn't come to see me before now.

When it came right down to it, I didn't want to lie to Mrs. Stuldy.

I let her into the house and she eased herself down onto the Marcuses' couch, and the whole time she was talking.

"I'm so glad I found you at home. I wasn't sure . . . Have you heard from Mrs. Marcus?"

"Uh, no," I said. A little shiver of fear seemed to flow through my whole body. I struggled to keep it out of my voice. "Why would I?"

"Oh, no, that's what I was afraid of," Mrs. Stuldy said. "I could hear your phone ringing from my house—sometimes I can, when the air-conditioning's off—and I could tell nobody was answering it, and I didn't know if you had an answering machine or not and I thought you probably hadn't heard—"

"Heard what?" I interrupted.

She peered at me with such sorrow in her expression that I immediately thought of all the worst possibilities. Had something happened to Mom or Bran?

But why would Mrs. Marcus have called? Why would Mrs. Stuldy be the one telling me the bad news?

Mrs. Stuldy cleared her throat.

"It's Mr. Marcus," she said. "He's dead."

23

"What?" I said.

"Mr. Marcus died. Yesterday," Mrs. Stuldy repeated.

And then the news sank in and I couldn't say anything. All the awful stories Bran had told me seemed to melt away, and all I could think about was the man from the family pictures. "Goofy Pop-Pop" was gone. He'd never clown around with his grandchildren again, never hold them on his lap and make them laugh.

He'd never make up with Mom or love me and Bran.

My eyes filled with tears.

"There, there," Mrs. Stuldy said, patting my hand. "Haven't you known anyone dead before?"

Silently I shook my head. I was afraid Mrs. Stuldy would say, *You didn't really even know him. You only saw him once.* But she didn't. She just sat there patting my hand. It was amazingly comforting, the feel of Mrs. Stuldy's warm, wrinkled skin.

Then a horrible thought struck me.

"Did—did Mrs. Marcus call you?" I wanted to ask what else they'd talked about, if Mrs. Stuldy had said anything about my family, about Bran's alleged house-sitting.

And was that awful of me, to worry about such a thing when Mr. Marcus was dead?

But Mrs. Stuldy was shaking her head.

"Oh, no," she said. "I just read it in the paper."

And for the first time I noticed that she was clutching a newspaper, folded over the wrong way to reveal an inside page. She held it out to me.

"I always read the obituaries first," she said. "You get to be my age, that's where you find the people you know. All the people in the rest of the paper seem so young—children, almost."

I glanced down at the newspaper. The words seemed to jump out at me: *John Marcus, 67, of Gulfstone and Opal, New York, died Tuesday at Binghamton Hospital, Binghamton, New York. . . .*

There was a picture, too, of Mr. Marcus as a much younger man. The picture was probably thirty years old. That was probably the way Mom remembered him.

I peered at the picture, trying to see hints in his bland face of the kind of man who'd burn his daughter's belongings, who'd destroy her diary and dreams. I tried to see hints too of the "Goofy Pop-Pop" he'd eventually become, or of the tired-looking old man I'd met at the beginning of the summer. But the picture was just ink on paper, a bad reproduction. And the man himself was gone.

I read the rest of the obituary in spurts, because I didn't seem capable of taking in more than one sentence at a time. Mr. Marcus had been a salesman, it said. He'd worked for the same company for forty-five years. He'd served in the army; he'd been a Jaycee. Then there was one sentence that left me feeling like I'd been punched in the stomach: *He is survived by his wife, Mary; one son, Michael, of Binghamton, New York; one daughter, Susan Bridgeman, of Portland, Oregon; and five grandchildren.*

Why were newspapers allowed to lie like that? I wanted to yell at the obituary, *You left out a few people. What about the other daughter, Becky Lassiter of Gulfstone? And he didn't have five grandchildren. He had seven.*

But probably the family had told the newspaper how many children and grandchildren he had. And the family said we didn't exist.

"I wonder how Mary's coping with all of this?" Mrs. Stuldy was saying. "There was one woman who really depended on her husband. . . . Maybe I should call her."

"What?" I said, suddenly jolted out of my fog and confusion. "You'd call her at a time like this?"

I wasn't crafty enough to try to dissuade her. I was just stunned. I looked up at Mrs. Stuldy's kind, sad face, and I felt like I was looking at the end of everything.

But, incredibly, she was tilting her head to the side. Reconsidering.

"You're right, honey. I wasn't thinking. That woman's dealing with funeral arrangements and kin flying in from all over the place. . . . When is the funeral? I forgot to look—they're not having a memorial service down here, too, are they?"

My heart seemed to skip a beat, but I forced myself to calmly bend my head over the newspaper again.

"'Services will be Thursday at Burkline Funeral Home in Binghamton, with burial to follow,'" I read out loud. I looked back at Mrs. Stuldy. "It doesn't say anything about a service in Gulfstone, just that memorial contributions can be made to the American Heart Association. If it's the heart association—does that mean he had a bad heart?"

What a stupid question. Of course he'd had a bad heart.

He'd disowned his own daughter. And then died without making up with her.

I couldn't understand why I was suddenly so angry.

"I think he'd had a heart attack or two," Mrs. Stuldy said vaguely. "But that was years ago, before they moved down here. He always seemed—fine. Or maybe not this past winter . . . Now that I think of it, he didn't do as much outdoors as he used to. This was the first year he didn't cut the grass himself when they were in town."

So Bran arrived at the Marcuses' at the exact right time, I thought. That seemed to fit Bran's argument that everything was meant to be.

But why was Mr. Marcus meant to die now? I wondered. *Now when I'd just found out who he was?*

"Maybe he was feeling poorly this past winter and just never told," Mrs. Stuldy was saying. "But . . . he was a young man, really. Just sixty-seven . . . I passed that birthday more than a decade ago."

I hadn't realized Mrs. Stuldy was so old, that she and Mr. Marcus were nearly part of different generations. She was staring off over my shoulder in a way that scared me.

"That doesn't mean you're going to die!" I said.

Mrs. Stuldy looked back at me.

"Oh, it happens to all of us eventually. I just want to see Sam out of jail first. . . ."

Had Mr. Marcus ever said, "I know I'll die someday. I just want to see Becky and her kids first?" Why hadn't those other heart attacks scared him into making up with Mom?

Mrs. Stuldy was still talking.

"I'm sure Mary will be getting in touch with you—with

your brother, I mean. She and John used to joke that if anything ever happened to him, she'd put the house down here on the market the next day. She was always bugging him to sell. She hated being so far away from her grandkids all winter. But he said they had to come for the sake of her health—she has some health problems too, though I'm not sure I ever heard exactly what they were. . . ."

It was hard to hear Mrs. Stuldy's voice through the buzzing in my ears. But the "she'd put the house on the market the next day" came through loud and clear, like an alarm clock going off in the middle of a confusing dream. I didn't have time to sit here grieving for Mr. Marcus, thinking about might have beens, worrying about Mrs. Marcus dying too. If Mrs. Marcus was going to sell our house, Bran needed to know that right away. We needed to move right away.

I sprang up.

"Mrs. Stuldy, I'm sorry—I don't mean to be rude, but—I need to go tell my brother about Mr. Marcus. I need to tell him now."

She blinked at me in surprise, a confused old lady. Somehow finding out about Mr. Marcus's death made her seem older and more fragile than ever, like an antique teacup you'd hide up on a shelf after all the other teacups are broken. I hated being so mean to her, but I couldn't let myself think about her feelings.

"I'll have to lock up," I said. "You have to leave too."

"Oh," she said. "Oh, dear. Well, of course I'll go. I wasn't thinking."

And then it was agonizing, waiting for her to slowly rise up from the couch, slowly shuffle over to the door. I should have walked her to her house, should have let her lean on my arm in that gap of empty space between the Marcuses' porch railing and her own. But I didn't. I didn't even watch to make sure she got home safely. I vaulted off the porch and jumped on my bike and pedaled off furiously toward the Shrimp Shack.

24

I'd never been to Bran's restaurant before,

but I'd been past it plenty of times. It was right downtown, in a large pink stucco building that looked about as much like a shack as Miss America looked like me. I chained my bike to a parking meter and raced inside.

"Where's Bran? Can you tell me where I can find Bran Lassiter?" I panted to the hostess.

She slowly turned the page of a fashion magazine before looking up.

"Bran? You mean that cute busboy who never talks? He's somewhere in the back."

"Thanks," I said, and ran past her, almost knocking over a waitress with a tray full of water glasses.

I pushed through a pair of swinging doors marked EMPLOYEES ONLY.

"Hey!" a man yelled behind me. "No customers allowed."

"I'm not a customer," I said. "I'm looking for my brother."

And then I saw Bran. He was chopping lettuce at a long, stainless steel counter.

"Bran, I've got to talk to you," I said.

Bran looked from me to the man behind me.

"Is it important?" Bran asked slowly. "I'm not due for a break any time soon—"

"Oh, go ahead," the man said. "We don't have any customers waiting. Next year, I won't be so stupid—I'm closing up for the off-season, like everyone else."

Still, Bran hesitated.

"Go on," the man said. "Your sister's acting like there's a death in the family or something."

I wanted so badly to say, *How did you know? That's exactly what happened.* I let the solemn words flow over me: "a death in the family." Did it still count as a death in the family if the family didn't count us?

I waited while Bran peeled off his rubber gloves and washed his hands. Then he led me out to a loading dock at the back of the restaurant.

"Is it Mom?" he asked. "Is she okay?"

"No, no, it's not her," I said impatiently. "It's Mr. Marcus. Mrs. Studly just told me—he died. Our grandfather died."

It was the first time I'd said the words out loud, together. I felt a little foolish, like I was claiming something that didn't really belong to me. But I also felt sadder. My grandfather had died.

Bran's face didn't change.

"So?" he said.

"So don't you feel sad? Aren't you even a little sorry that he and Mom are never going to make up?"

Bran just looked at me.

"Britt," he said gently. "They were never going to make up anyway."

"But—" I blinked back tears.

"Come on, Britt," Bran said. "Why should you care? *I* don't. This is like—like Hitler dying. Do you think people cried over Hitler?"

I wanted to defend Mr. Marcus, my grandfather, but of course I couldn't. I swallowed hard.

"You ought to care," I said. "Mrs. Marcus is probably going to sell the house now, and you know the Realtor or whoever will find out that we're living there. So we'll have to tell Mom and move."

This was what I had wanted to tell Bran so urgently, but I tried to sound casual and offhand. Like I wasn't dying to tell, dying to move.

Bran frowned.

"Just 'probably'?" he asked, like a debater finding a weak point in an argument.

I wanted to say, No—definitely. There's a Realtor coming tomorrow at nine A.M. I wanted Bran to see how urgent this was. But I forced myself to be honest.

"Well," I said slowly. "Mrs. Stuldy said Mrs. Marcus always joked that if Mr. Marcus died, she'd put the house on the market the next day. Mrs. Marcus didn't like coming down here and being away from—from her grandkids." That was hard to say, and I stopped talking.

"That's just talk, then," Bran said. "Nobody would sell a house the day after its owner died. There are a lot of decisions involved in selling a house, a lot of paperwork. When did Mr. Marcus die?"

I noticed Bran didn't call him, "our grandfather."

"Yesterday," I said in a trembling voice. "He died yesterday."

"Then Mrs. Marcus is busy with the funeral and everything," Bran said. "And mourning. My boss's father died last week, and he was just saying today that his mother can't even pick out her own clothes anymore, she's so blown away by

159

grief. Probably Mrs. Marcus will be like that—even if she does sell the house, she wouldn't do it for months. And we'd be gone by then."

How could Bran sound so cheerful about other people's grief?

"But we don't *know* that," I said. "We don't want to take any chances, do we?"

My question seemed to hover in the air between us. And for a moment it was like I'd torn away Bran's mask and could see beyond his confidence and his bravado, even beyond his anger. I could see he wished he'd never found the Marcuses, never offered to mow their yard, never told Mom we could move into their house. I could see he knew—even more than I did—what a huge chance we'd been taking all along.

"We don't have much choice," Bran said grimly. "We can't move now. Mom's got exams next week."

And for some reason I thought about Mrs. Stuldy's son then. Sam. Was there some point, when he was robbing the bank, when he thought, *Oh, no, this was all a big mistake. But I can't back out now?* Once he was at the bank, once he was pointing the gun, did he think he had any other choice but to pull the trigger?

"Bran," I said. "There was this girl at school last year. I didn't really know her, but everybody said she and her family were living in their car. In the school parking lot. The principal let them stay there. If we had to, we could do that. Just until the fall. It wouldn't kill us."

Bran winced.

"It would kill Mom," he said. "That's the kind of thing her parents told her would happen if she even dated Dad. And there are laws about that. We could be arrested for vagrancy or loitering. . . . We couldn't do it. If we move out of the Marcuses' house, Mom will have to drop out of school."

And then it was those words that hung in the hot, stale air on that loading dock.

"What if Mom sees the newspaper?" I asked. "What if she reads Mr. Marcus's obituary and figures everything out?"

Bran waved away that concern.

"Mom won't read the newspaper," Bran said. "She hasn't read anything but textbooks in two months." He patted my shoulder. "Don't worry, Britt. Everything's going to be all right. Mrs. Marcus is up in New York and her husband just died and she's not thinking about the house down here at all. Okay?"

Bran smiled at me, his mask of confidence firmly back in place.

"Mmm," I said, not committing myself. I couldn't promise not to worry.

"Just keep hanging around Mrs. Stuldy," Bran said. "If she tells you anything definite, let me know."

What could be more definite than death?

"I'd better get back to work now," Bran said. "If I got fired, we'd really be in trouble!"

He gave me a grin that was totally fake. And then he was gone.

I didn't follow him back through the restaurant. I just stood there, breathing in the smell of rotting garbage from the Dumpster a few feet away. I hadn't noticed the odor before when I was talking to Bran. But now I realized the entire loading dock reeked. So did the alley it faced—the alley was positively studded with Dumpsters. I jumped down from the loading dock and looked to the right and the left, trying to find a way out of the alley. But none of the stores and restaurants looked the same from the back as they had from the front. The fronts had been polished, scrubbed, proper. The backs were dirty, ramshackle, garbage strewn. Were people like that too, always putting a good face on shameful secrets? Was Mrs. Stuldy the only exception, because she didn't hide her shame?

I thought about Mr. Marcus's funeral up in New York. Everybody would probably talk about what a great person he was, what a great father and grandfather he was. Probably nobody would mention the daughter and grandchildren he'd so cruelly disowned.

And then there was Bran. Everyone at the restaurant undoubtedly thought he was the most conscientious kid on the planet, not wanting to stop chopping lettuce even for a second to talk to his sister. Nobody knew he'd been lying all summer. No one knew he'd deceived his grandparents, stolen their key, broken into their house.

And what about me? From one side I probably looked like a loyal kid sister, not tattling on Bran. From the other side—was I an accomplice to a crime?

I wanted so badly to tell Mom everything, let her figure out for herself what to do, even if it meant she dropped out of school. But then I thought about how Bran had looked just before he'd answered my question "We don't want to take any chances, do we?" At that moment he'd looked so vulnerable, so lost, that all I wanted to do was protect him.

It was so backward, me protecting Bran, him protecting Mom.

As soon as I stumbled out of that alley, I got my bike and rode straight to Mrs. Stuldy's.

25

"**Can I ask you a question about your**
son without you thinking I'm like the women down at the senior center who talk mean about you behind your back?" I asked
Mrs. Stuldy all in one breath, as soon as I'd settled in at her
kitchen table.

Mrs. Stuldy blinked a few times and poured me a glass of milk.

"Of course," she said. "I know you're not like that."

I wanted to savor the feeling that gave me, the sense that she
trusted me. But I pushed on with my question.

"Before Sam was arrested," I said, "but after he'd, you know,
killed that man . . . if you'd have known what he did, would you
have told on him? Would you have turned him in to the cops?"

Mrs. Stuldy stared at me across her red-checked tablecloth,
and for a minute I thought she hadn't heard my question. Or
hadn't understood it. I was trying to think how to rephrase it a
little more gently when she whispered, "Oh, honey, I am so glad
I didn't know. So glad I didn't have to make that decision."

I wanted to keep asking, to keep peppering her with what ifs.
But I already felt like I'd beaten her up just with that one question. I took a drink of milk.

Mrs. Stuldy was squinting at me.

"You don't—you don't think John Marcus was *murdered*, do
you?" she asked.

"Oh, no. It's not that," I said. "Not at all."

And then I felt a little better, because at least Bran's secret wasn't that bad. It wasn't murder.

Mrs. Stuldy chuckled a little.

"Roy keeps telling me I watch too many police shows on TV," she said. "Makes me morbid." A shadow crossed her face, and I knew she was thinking she had reason to be. Then she shrugged. "It doesn't do any good to sit around thinking about bad things. I tell you what. Why don't you go down to Eckerd's and pick out a nice sympathy card for me to send to Mary. I'll mix us up some sweets. Maybe those chocolate-oatmeal no-bake cookies. That way I won't have to turn on the oven. I just didn't feel like baking early this morning after I found out about John. But there's nothing like chocolate for cheering a body up."

"Oh, no!" I said, too loudly. I gulped. "I mean, you don't have to make anything for me."

"But I want to," Mrs. Stuldy said, and reached back to the kitchen counter to get her purse.

I'd really wanted to say, "Oh, no, you can't send a sympathy card." I hadn't known I'd have to worry about that, too. But of course Mrs. Stuldy would want to send a card. And Mrs. Marcus would want to know that Mrs. Stuldy was sorry about Mr. Marcus dying.

"Here," Mrs. Stuldy said, pulling a handful of dollar bills from her purse. "Three for the card, and four for you for running my errand."

"Can't Mr. Stuldy do it for you?" I said. My voice came out sounding tortured. "Something like that's awfully personal."

And then I was furious with myself, because if Mr. Stuldy

picked out the card I wouldn't be around to see if Mrs. Stuldy wrote anything about us in it.

Mrs. Stuldy held the money back for a moment.

"Oh, I forgot, you've never known anyone who died before. I can kind of remember being squeamish about death myself when I was your age. But really, picking out a sympathy card is no different than choosing any other kind of card. That's why Roy can't do it for me. You know, for my birthday last year he found something with orange and black elephants on it. I swear. Uglier than a mud fence. I figure he must have asked for it special. *I* didn't mind, but for the Marcuses . . . Get something with flowers on it, and a nice verse. Something real pretty."

She held out the money to me, and I didn't know what else to do but to take it.

I stood in the greeting card aisle of Eckerd's forever, rejecting one card after another. I'd think about how the card could be the end of us living in the Marcuses' house, and I'd want to bolt out of Eckerd's right then, no matter what Mrs. Stuldy wanted. But then I'd think about how bad Mrs. Stuldy felt for Mrs. Marcus, and how I'd want as many sympathy cards as possible if I were Mrs. Marcus.

I felt like I deserved a sympathy card or two myself.

In the end I picked out a card with a single rose on the front. On the inside it said, *Thinking of you in your time of sorrow.* I suspected Mrs. Stuldy would have preferred something with frillier words and a frillier picture, but she wasn't doing the picking. I was.

And then I stood there for a moment longer, and my hand reached out for a card I'd glanced at and put back once or twice already. It was much too plain for Mrs. Stuldy's taste. It just said, *In Sympathy* in gold on the front, and then, *You are in our prayers* on the inside. And that was it—no pictures, no flowers, nothing else. I pulled out an envelope to go with it, and then I carried both cards up to the cash register.

"Ring these up separately, please," I told the cashier.

I could send Mrs. Marcus a card too, I decided. Bran and Mom and I had never been very religious, but "you are in our prayers" seemed like the right message. I couldn't figure out how the Marcuses could have been so horrible to Mom and look so kind and loving in their family pictures. I couldn't figure out if I was doing the right thing by protecting Bran even though both of us knew it was wrong for us to live in the Marcuses' house. I didn't know how I could carry the rose card back to Mrs. Stuldy's house, knowing it might be the end of Bran's secret. But I thought maybe God could understand everything.

It seemed like a good time for praying.

I walked back to Mrs. Stuldy's house and showed her the rose card. She gave a little grunt that was probably disappointment but said, "That's real fine. Kind of classy. Now, can you open it up and write what I tell you to write?"

She was handing me the pen. I looked up at her in surprise. She sighed.

"My hands shake too bad," she said. "Look." She turned over the sales slip I'd given her, and painstakingly wrote something on the back. Then she held the paper out for me to see. It looked like a child had been scribbling with one of those vibrating pens. I couldn't make out a single letter.

"Uh, is that—"

"It's my signature," Mrs. Stuldy said. "Couldn't tell, could you? My son's about the only person in the world who can read my writing. It's funny—when I was a girl I had the best penmanship in the whole class. And, you know, I hated to cook back then. When Roy married me I didn't feed him a decent meal for twenty years. But right after . . . after Sam went to jail, my hands started shaking, and the doctors could never give me enough medicine to stop it. Seemed like the only thing my hands were good for anymore was stirring. So that's what I did. Cooking, baking . . . I even got so I liked it. Now. You gonna write in that card for me or am I going to have to send it out with Roy's chicken scratchings on it? He was always the worst in penmanship, even seventy years ago."

"Uh, okay. I can write for you," I said, reaching for the pen. I had the feeling Mrs. Stuldy was trying to tell me about more than her handwriting, but my thoughts were too jumbled to listen well.

I gripped the pen and prepared to form my letters carefully. "'Dear Mary,'" Mrs. Stuldy dictated. "'We were real sorry to hear about John. We'll be praying for you.'" She paused for a minute. "Do you want to say something about how you're writing this for me, and you're sorry too? Seeing as how you were so sad this morning—"

"No, that's okay," I said, too quickly. "I got a card for Mom and Bran and me to send. See?" I pulled out the bag I'd tucked under my chair. "This rose card should just be from you and Mr. Stuldy."

My heart was pounding so loudly I was sure Mrs. Stuldy would hear it. But she just shrugged.

"You're right, I wasn't thinking. Of course you got a card of your own," she said. "You're a good child, you know that? You can just sign it, now, 'Sincerely, Roy and Early Stuldy.' No point in writing a lot on a condolences card. People don't want to have to read too much through their tears."

Slowly, slowly, I let out the breath I'd been holding. Bran and Mom and I were safe again after all.

For now.

I wrote out the Marcuses' New York address on both envelopes, and then Mrs. Stuldy insisted on giving me a stamp for my card as well as hers.

"Call it a tip," she said cheerfully. "Now, are you ready for the cookies?"

She did indeed have a plateful sitting on the counter. And the whole kitchen smelled warm and chocolaty. But my stomach churned at the thought of any food, and I was too antsy to sit there leisurely eating cookies and chatting with Mrs. Stuldy.

"Thanks, but I think I'd better go ahead and mail these cards," I said. "And I should check in with my other customers. I've been neglecting them lately."

"All right," Mrs. Stuldy said wistfully. "I'll just wrap up some cookies to send with you."

I dropped the cookies off at home, then I walked on up to the mailbox two blocks away. I still hadn't written anything on my card for Mrs. Marcus. I took a pen with me, and then I stood at the mailbox with the card open on the top, the pen in my hand.

I certainly didn't plan to sign my name, but what did I want to say to my grandmother after all these years? What could I say?

The heat pressed in on me. I was like some statue: Girl Who

Can't Decide by Mailbox. It seemed like hours passed before I finally folded the card into the envelope and sealed it and stuffed it into the mailbox without writing anything. The preprinted *You are in our prayers* was the best I could do.

I just wondered. Were we ever in Mrs. Marcus's prayers?

26

Bran came home after work and didn't
say a word to me about Mr. Marcus dying or us moving or anything like that. He acted like nothing had changed. And I guess
for him, it hadn't.

But I spent an hour that night staring at the "Goofy Pop-
Pop" picture and crying. It was like my own private memorial
service.

The next day, after Mom and Bran left, I unlocked Bran's
closet and pulled out the box of pictures once again. This
time I stared at all the pictures of Mrs. Marcus: her kissing
Mr. Marcus under the mistletoe; her laughing as a young
mother, a baby and a toddler in her arms; her proudly arrang-
ing her daughter Susan's wedding veil; her walking on the
beach with Mr. Marcus, each of them holding a grandchild's
hand. "I'm very sorry for your loss," I whispered to each picture—a phrase I'd picked up from the Eckerd's sympathy card
aisle.

For that short period of time I didn't let myself think about
what the pictures left out. About *who* they left out.

But after that I was able to go back to my usual routine, my
usual circuit between Winn-Dixie and Eckerd's, carrying milk
and bread and Tums and the *National Enquirer*s for my neighbors. I bought sympathy cards for Mrs. Marcus on behalf of

two other neighbors, and wrote their messages as well. Mr. Johnson said his eyes were too weak; Mrs. Zendt blamed her arthritis. Secretly I wondered if it was just that they each wanted to keep death as far away from themselves as they could.

At least with me writing the cards for them, I knew they didn't say anything about Bran house-sitting.

And then somehow June melted into July and we were still living in the Marcuses' house. Nobody caught us. No Realtors showed up, and neither did the police. I began to think that maybe Bran was right, that we could go the whole summer without being detected.

I could still hear the voice inside me insisting, *No, no, this is wrong. You've got to tell Mom!* But I kept holding up that voice against images in my head: Bran's look of panic and fear and dread on the Shrimp Shack loading dock when I'd asked, "We don't want to take any chances, do we?"; Mom's face just seconds away from dissolving into tears at dinner the night I'd asked, "Do you have any happy memories of your parents?"

I carried around other voices in my head too: Bran saying, "Think about it all summer long, if you want"; Mrs. Stuldy telling me the first time I met her, "Life's too short to take a long time making decisions."

I was still the Girl Who Can't Decide statue. I was just a statue who moved around, looking like an ordinary twelve-year-old to all the rest of the world.

Why couldn't anyone see how upset and worried and terrified and troubled and sad and confused and lonely and grieving and guilty and longing and helpless and hopeful I was under my skin?

I think Mrs. Stuldy came the closest to knowing that

something was wrong. Sometimes she seemed to be watching me carefully, her eyes as sharp as a bird's.

"Are you all right?" she asked me out of the blue one morning as I sat in her kitchen eating apple crumb cake. "Walking around so much in all this heat—it can't be healthy for you."

She'd never acted worried about the heat before.

"I'm fine," I said, as cheerfully as I could.

She sighed.

"That's what Sam said the night before he was arrested."

"I'm not—I mean—" I was flustered then. What if Mrs. Stuldy somehow managed to guess everything?

Mrs. Stuldy sighed again.

"Oh, don't worry. I know you haven't murdered anybody. I'm just a foolish old woman who's seen too many things go wrong. I know when I was a girl I'd brood for days over nothing—like whether Herman Hinkerman was making goo-goo eyes at me or at Mildred Stollins. And now Herman and Mildred have both been dead more than fifty years. Herman was in World War Two, you know, and . . ."

I let her talk, though I wanted so badly to tell her I wasn't just brooding over nothing.

"What would you have done, about Sam, I mean, if you'd known that everything wasn't fine?" I asked when she was done with her story. "Before he was arrested, I mean?"

Mrs. Stuldy frowned thoughtfully.

"I don't reckon there was anything I could have done," she said. "Except keep loving him. And maybe started trying even sooner to forgive him."

I thought maybe that was her answer, a few weeks late, to

my question about whether she would have turned Sam in.

"How long ago was that?" I asked, still curious. "How long has Sam been in prison?"

She gazed off over my shoulder, and seemed to be counting in her head. I thought she was adding up days, tallying up months. But then she answered: "Twenty years."

"Twenty years?" I repeated in amazement. I wouldn't have guessed even twenty months. I peered off into her crowded living room. "And you've been holding on to his furniture for him all that time?"

"Yep," Mrs. Stuldy said, sounding a little surprised herself.

And then I thought that if I could tell her everything, Mrs. Stuldy would understand completely about me being the Girl Who Can't Decide. Mrs. Stuldy was like that too.

But of course I couldn't tell her anything.

July inched along, a blur of heat and worry and long, punishing trips between the neighborhood and Winn-Dixie and Eckerd's. And then suddenly Mom's exams were over and she had three days off as a break between summer sessions.

"Let's go to the beach," she proposed at breakfast the morning of her first day off. "Just the three of us."

"I can't," Bran said nervously, cutting his eyes toward me. "I have to work."

"Then it's ladies only," Mom said. "What about it, Britt? Sun and surf and sand, and nothing to do except apply suntan lotion, all day long."

"Um, sure," I said. "Sounds like fun."

But I could tell my voice was a little off, like I was trying too hard to sound delighted. Bran frowned at me from across the table, sending silent messages: *Act normal* and *Don't tell her anything* and *Remember not to ask about her parents* and *Protect her, please protect her.* . . .

Then Bran left for work, and it felt surreal, Mom and me rushing around getting ready for the beach. I could tell Mom wanted to re-create the carefree day we'd had at the beginning of the summer, but I couldn't quite get in the right mood. I realized I'd been relying on all those long, hot, punishing walks. I didn't think I deserved any fun.

"Noodle fight!" Mom yelled, springing out of the laundry room with two long foam beach toys that belonged to the Marcuses. "Want the yellow 'sword' or the blue one?"

She stood in mock fighting stance, holding the noodles like weapons.

"Uh, Mom, I don't think we should do that indoors," I said. "We might break something."

"You've turned into as big a spoilsport as Bran," she said, dropping the noodles onto the table. She looked at me a little more closely. "You aren't mad at me, are you, because I haven't been able to spend much time with you lately?"

"No, of course not," I said stiffly.

"Once this summer's over, I won't take such an intense load of classes," she said. "So it's not like you're losing your mother permanently. I know . . . I know this summer's been hard on you, and I do appreciate all the sacrifices you've made. Like having your own mother forget your name—let's see, it's Bridget, isn't it?"

She made a goofy face at me, like she was begging me to giggle and clown around with her. I forced myself to pick up a noodle and halfheartedly bop her on the shoulder with it.

"Wrong answer! You're sentenced to eight hours in the

broiling sun!" I proclaimed, trying as hard as I could to sound mock serious and lighthearted and happy.

I'm not sure she quite fell for it, but she giggled as she dashed back to her room to change into her swimsuit.

I put the noodles by the door, on top of our huge tote bag of towels, sunscreen, chips, and soda. I tried not to think about the pictures I'd seen of Marcus grandchildren floating on top of these very noodles, or brandishing them like swords of their own.

Instead I focused on what I'd say if I were the old Britt, ignorant and protected, not trying to protect anyone else.

"Mom, why'd you have to let Bran have the car today?" I called. "We're going to be too worn out to swim once we carry all this down to the beach."

"Who said anything about swimming?" Mom hollered back. "I'm just going to bask in the sun all day."

"Then I'll bury you in sand," I threatened.

So far I was doing okay, but could I really keep this up for eight hours?

The noodles slipped off the tote bag and I bent down to put them back. I was straightening up when I heard a key in the door and saw the door handle turning.

My first thought was, *Oh, Bran got off so he can come to the beach too.* I hadn't heard the car, but the air-conditioning was on, its subtle hum reminding me, as always, that we were breathing the Marcuses' air. I felt a surge of relief. If Bran came along, he could act normal for both of us. I lifted a noodle, ready to hit him playfully when he walked in.

Then the door opened. It wasn't Bran.

I recognized the face from hundreds of pictures I'd pored

over. But she looked older now. The lines in her cheeks were deeper; her white hair drooped across her forehead, instead of rising gracefully the way I'd seen it so many times.

"Mrs. Marcus?" I said uncertainly. Then I whispered, "Grammy?"

Mrs. Marcus shrieked.

"Who are you?" she asked. "What are you doing in my house?"

I dropped the noodle and reached out to her. I think I just wanted to calm her down, but she jerked away.

She was scared of me.

"It's all right," I said, trying to sound comforting. "I know you didn't expect anyone to be here. And I know we really shouldn't be here but . . . Well, it's not as bad as it seems. I'm your granddaughter."

I fixed her with a crooked smile, like a gift. A gift with a message attached: *Hello, Grandmother-I've-never-met. Why don't you love me? Can't you start loving me now?*

Mrs. Marcus drew herself up straight, with great dignity.

"You are *not* my granddaughter. I've heard about people like you—trying to prey on an old woman's confusion. Well, I am not confused, so don't even try it."

"No, really—," I started to explain, but Mrs. Marcus was looking past me. She let out another shriek.

"What have you done to my house?"

I turned around and followed her gaze. The living room was a little messy, but only because we'd been getting ready. I'd left a T-shirt hanging half off the coffee table. One of Mom's textbooks was open on the couch. And of course all Mrs. Marcus's pictures were missing; every personal touch that said, "The Marcuses live here" had vanished.

I wanted to assure her they were only hidden, not stolen, but there wasn't time.

Mom was coming around the corner from the hall.

Her bright orange swimsuit glowed against her pale skin. She'd pulled her blond hair back into a ponytail. She was beautiful, as perfect as a Barbie doll. I was proud of her. I looked back at Mrs. Marcus, waiting for the cries of recognition. I held my breath. They would hug, of course, and cry, and try to explain. There'd probably be a few minutes when they forgot I was even there. But that was okay. They needed—I thought of the term the talk shows always used—they needed time to heal.

Mom was looking blankly at Mrs. Marcus.

"Is this one of the neighbors you've been helping, Britt?" Mom asked. "Can you introduce us? I'm sorry I haven't been very neighborly—I've been studying so hard this summer—"

"I am *not* a neighbor! This is my house!" Mrs. Marcus exploded.

Mom looked at me in confusion. I stared back, just as confused. Had Mom and Mrs. Marcus really changed that much in eighteen years that they didn't even recognize each other?

"Mom, this is your mother!" I said. "And Mrs. Marcus, this is your daughter. Becky. I know you disowned her, but still—can't you forgive her? Don't you recognize her?" Both Mom and Mrs. Marcus were staring at me in disbelief. I wasn't saying things right. What would Bran do? I desperately needed his help. I edged toward the phone. "I think Bran ought to come home," I muttered.

Mom was still gaping at me. Mrs. Marcus recovered her voice more quickly.

"Get out of my house!" she screamed.

Mom and I looked at each other helplessly. I punched numbers on the phone without looking. Mom stepped forward.

"Mrs. Marquis?" she said hesitantly. "I don't know why my daughter's saying that. There's some sort of mix-up here. But I'm Bran Lassiter's mother. He's your house-sitter, remember?" Her voice was high and unnatural. She was treating Mrs. Marcus like some senile old lady. I knew from Mrs. Stuldy that old people hate that.

"I don't have a house-sitter!" Mrs. Marcus yelled. "Just a yard boy, and his name is Brian, and he *wasn't* supposed to come into the house—"

"Oh, but that's—" I wanted to explain how Brian the yard boy was really Bran, and why he'd had to lie about his name. But just then I heard Bran's "Hello?" on the phone, and I hissed at him instead: "Mrs. Marcus is here! She and Mom are acting like they don't even know each other!" I ran my words together because I didn't want to miss hearing anything that Mom and Mrs. Marcus said.

"What?" Bran said on the other end of the line, sounding much farther away than ten blocks.

"Come home right now! It's an emergency!" I shouted back, and hung up without waiting for his answer.

Mom took another tentative step toward Mrs. Marcus.

"Do you want to sit down?" she asked Mrs. Marcus cautiously. "I'm sure we can talk this out. You hired my son Bran to take care of your house while you were away. Not just the yard, the whole house. And it's Bran, not Brian. And Bran told you—or Mr. Marquis, anyway—that my daughter, Brittany, and I would be staying here with him. I talked about everything with your husband. Is he here with you? Surely he can straighten everything out—"

"My husband is dead," Mrs. Marcus said icily. She did not sit down.

"Oh," Mom said, momentarily taken aback.

"Mr. Marcus died last month, Mom," I said. "Your father. I'm sorry. Bran and I should have told you." I frowned. It did seem so clear suddenly, that we ought to have told. This was a horrible way for Mom to find out about her father's death. "I'm sorry," I said again. "And it really wasn't Mr. Marcus that you talked to back in the spring. It was someone Bran knew from school."

Mom looked back and forth between me and Mrs. Marcus like we were both total lunatics. She seemed to be wondering if she could believe anything either of us said.

"Well," she said. "Mr. Marquis didn't mention that anyone would be coming back at all this summer, so that's why we're a little surprised. . . . Perhaps you weren't aware of the full extent of the arrangement your husband made with my son, but I can assure you we have every right to be here. Perhaps if you think back you'll remember. . . ."

A tiny part of me was impressed that Mom could forge ahead, continuing that calm, soothing flow of words. I could imagine her as a doctor talking to a mental patient, with just that tone. But to her own mother? Maybe that was the problem. Maybe both of her parents had been crazy.

"You—you—," Mrs. Marcus sputtered angrily. "How dare you—"

I couldn't stand it.

"Why are you both acting like this?" I screamed. "Why can't you just make up?"

Mrs. Marcus glared at me.

"I don't have to put up with this! I'm calling the police!" she announced.

Instinctively I laid my hand over the phone. Mrs. Marcus leaned forward, like she was going to come over and grab the phone from me, then she seemed to change her mind. She whirled around and walked back through the door.

"Mrs. Marcus, wait!" I started to run after her, but Mom grabbed my arm and stopped me.

"Hold it right there, young lady," she said. "I don't want you chasing her and terrifying her totally out of her wits. If she calls the police—if she's even Mrs. Marquis in the first place— Bran will straighten things out. You need to tell me—why did you say that woman was my mother?"

"Because she is!" Everything was so messed up, I couldn't help sobbing. I blubbered, "Why—didn't you—know her?" Then I was crying so hard I couldn't talk. I collapsed into a heap on the couch. Mom seemed to give up on making sense of anything I said and just sat beside me, patting my back.

And then Bran was there, and I was so relieved.

"Did you tell her off?" he asked Mom. "Ever since I tracked down your parents on the Internet, I've been imagining something like this—I wish I'd been here."

Suddenly I wondered: *Had Bran kind of wanted to get caught?*

I didn't have time to think about that. Mom looked from me to Bran, then said very quietly, "Explain."

Bran told Mom everything he'd told me, about searching the Internet, and finding out where our grandparents lived, and deciding that our grandparents owed us a summer without rent. He explained the Marquis/Marcus lie, the fake Mr.

Marquis on the phone, the extra mowing money that he'd said was for house-sitting. Through it all, Mom sat silently, listening, her fingers clutched over her own mouth. By the end, she had her entire face buried in her hands.

Then, when Bran stopped talking, she whispered without looking up, "You found the wrong Marcuses."

27

The house was so quiet we could hear a siren far off in the distance.

"What?" Bran said. "How could that be?"

"When I was a kid," Mom said, "there was another couple in town with the same name as my parents. John and Mary Marcus. They weren't related or anything, but my parents were always getting their mail and vice versa. The bank even got their accounts mixed up once, and that was a mess. Something about their social security numbers being similar too. The other Marcuses must have moved to New York after I left. And my parents didn't own their own property, they never had a listed phone number—you wouldn't have seen a trace of them. So you found the other Marcuses instead."

Bran was silent for a minute. Then he said, "Oh."

Mom started shaking her head violently.

"How could you, Bran?" She was still speaking quietly, but her voice was heavy. Screaming would have been easier to listen to. "I've always trusted you. I've always counted on you. What were you thinking? Even if you found the right family— even if they were the kind to own a house in Florida—did you really think I'd want to live in their house? To use something of theirs? Didn't you know how much I'd hate being beholden to them for anything?"

Mom stood up, her hands outstretched beseechingly.

"But Mom, they owe you—," Bran began.

Mom whirled around furiously, coming face-to-face with Bran.

"No, they do not! They don't owe me a thing, and I don't owe them anything either. That's the deal. Don't you see? I'm as happy to have them out of my life as they are to have me out of theirs. *That's* why I never said much about them. It was better to pretend they didn't exist."

"But kids need grandparents," I said in a small voice.

Now Mom glared at me. I sank lower into the couch.

"Sure, if they're good grandparents," Mom said. She was truly yelling now. "But guess what? This isn't a fairy tale. This is real life. Want to know the winners you got in the grandparents lottery? One set told their son, your father, to stop going to AA meetings because 'You're just a social drinker. What's wrong with that?' The other set—" Mom gulped back a sob. Tears glistened in her eyes. But she continued, her voice stronger than before. "Right after your father left me I sent a picture of you two to my parents. You were both so cute in that picture. You looked like angels. I thought, *If that doesn't bring them to their senses, nothing will.* But they sent back the letter without even opening it." The sob came out. She bit her lip and went on. "So I had to protect you. I wanted to raise you without being bitter—everything was my fault, so I wanted to save you two. But now—"

The sound of the siren got closer. Mom gasped.

"Oh, no. She did call the police. Of course she did. Why wouldn't she?" Mom looked around wildly, as if she was planning to grab our things and run. But signs of our presence were everywhere. It wasn't just my T-shirt on the coffee table and Mom's book on the couch—our possessions had settled over the Marcuses' like the layers of sedimentary rock we'd studied in science class. No wonder Mrs. Marcus had been horrified by the sight of her living room. It didn't look like she belonged here anymore. It looked like we did.

"Mom, don't you think we can explain—," Bran started.

"How? 'We didn't mean to break into a stranger's house. We really meant to steal from people who hate us'? I'm sure that'll go over really well." Now Mom sobbed for real. "I can't believe this. You're just like me. You made one mistake as a teenager that's going to ruin the rest of your life. You're going to have a criminal record. You might even go to jail. How do you think that looks on a college application?" Mom was hysterical. "Don't you know that every time I regretted my mistakes, I thought, It's all going to be worthwhile, because Bran and Brittany are such great kids. I'm so proud of them. I had this little dream. I thought when you two were all grown up and complete successes, I wanted to take you back to my parents and say, 'Look how wonderfully they turned out. You were so wrong.' And now I find out my parents were right. They always said, 'The sins of the fathers are visited on the sons.' And now my faults led to yours—"

We were so paralyzed listening to Mom cry, it took a while to realize that the siren had stopped. I went over and peeked out the front blinds, but there wasn't a police car in sight. What did they do—hide somewhere and wait for the criminals to come out? I knew that wasn't true, because all the police cars that came to Sunset Terrace had arrived with lights flashing and sirens blaring.

"Mom," I said hesitantly. "I don't think the police were coming here."

"Well, it's just a matter of time," she said bitterly.

"Mom," Bran protested. "Don't be like that—"

I couldn't stand any more of this. I slipped out the front door and slumped on the porch, my back against the wall, my face in my hands. Behind me, I could hear Mom and Bran shouting at each other. It was like being back at Sunset Terrace, listening to other people fight. But I'd always lain in bed then thinking, *I'm so glad my family's not like that.* Now it was my family. Out of habit I turned around, ready to run to Bran and say, *Make everything right again.* But this time he couldn't. He was the one who had made everything wrong.

I stared out at the deserted street, waiting for the police. Maybe I could explain everything when they came. Maybe they'd listen if I told them what a great person Bran really was, how he really didn't mean any harm, how he was just trying to help Mom. But why should they believe me? I was guilty too. More guilty, maybe—I'd known all along that what Bran did was wrong, and I didn't do anything about it.

I felt so awful then that I couldn't sit still. I stood up, and my feet carried me automatically down our sidewalk and over to the Stuldys'. I looked at every frond and flower along their driveway as if I'd never seen them before. The colors were too bright in the harsh sunlight. I felt like I was in one of those nightmares where everything was different—backward and topsy-turvy and upside down. Only this was real life. By the time I reached Mrs. Stuldy's porch, I was desperate for someone to comfort me. I pounded on the door.

"Mrs. Stuldy! It's me! Britt!"

"Come in!" she called from the back of the house.

I pushed my way in and dodged the extra furniture in the living room. I tried not to think about how all that furniture was there because Mrs. Stuldy's son was in prison, and maybe Bran would be going there too. I was panting and sweating when I got to the kitchen doorway.

And for the second time that day I came face-to-face with Mrs. Marcus.

"**You!**" Mrs. Marcus practically spat. She had a cup in her hand and it wobbled, sloshing tea onto the table.

I couldn't say anything. I squinted, confused. Not by Mrs. Marcus—by what I was feeling. I would have expected to be angry or scared, but the emotion I was flooded with was entirely different.

It was hope.

I didn't know why. It was like my body figured out something before my brain did.

"Glad you're here, Britt," Mrs. Stuldy said in her most comforting voice. "Sounds like you and Mrs. Marcus have something to work out."

I looked from Mrs. Stuldy to Mrs. Marcus, and suddenly I understood. This was our chance. If Mrs. Marcus hadn't called the police yet, maybe Mom or Bran could persuade her not to. Or if the police were already on the way, maybe we could talk Mrs. Marcus into not—what was it called?—pressing charges. I looked back, but the distance I'd have to travel to get back to Mom and Bran seemed impossible. And they were busy screaming at each other. Could either of them explain everything calmly to Mrs. Marcus? Bran was still too defensive. And Mom was still hoping that Mrs. Marcus herself was an impostor.

For the first time in my life, I felt like everything depended on me.

I slipped into a chair opposite Mrs. Marcus at the table.

"I—I'm sorry," I whispered. "About everything. But especially about—about Mr. Marcus dying." I hadn't planned to say that. It just came out. "I sent you a card. I just didn't write my name in it. I couldn't."

"That was you?" Mrs. Marcus said.

I thought how strange it must have seemed for Mrs. Marcus to get four cards addressed in the same hand, one unsigned.

"Britt here wrote out my card for me too," Mrs. Stuldy said. "She's been the best helper in the neighborhood this summer."

I could tell Mrs. Stuldy was trying to help me, but her voice boomed out so heartily that both Mrs. Marcus and I winced.

"Oh," Mrs. Marcus said stiffly, looking down at her tea.

I swallowed a lump in my throat.

"When Mrs. Stuldy showed me the obituary for Mr. Marcus, I felt really bad for you and your family," I said. "I saw some of your family pictures, and I could tell that you all loved each other a lot." Something caught in my throat, but I forced myself to keep talking. "And I felt sorry for myself, because I really did believe that Mr. Marcus was my grandfather. And that you were my grandmother."

Mrs. Stuldy must have been more shocked than anybody to hear that, but she didn't even blink. "And why was that, child?" she asked softly.

I didn't answer her right away. I appealed directly to Mrs. Marcus.

"I know now that I was wrong about being your granddaughter. I—I wish I were. But I know it must have really upset you to hear me say things like that. And to find Mom and Bran and me living in your house. I'm really sorry."

Mrs. Marcus accepted my apology with an impatient nod.

"I told you Britt was a good kid," Mrs. Stuldy said, a hint of triumph in her voice.

Mrs. Marcus didn't look convinced.

"So maybe you were misled," she said. "But surely your parents knew—"

"It's just my mother," I said softly. "And she didn't know anything about this. She thought Mr. Marcus really did hire Bran to house-sit, that we were protecting your house from thieves. Not—" I looked down. "Not breaking the law ourselves."

"But you were breaking the law," Mrs. Marcus exploded. "All of you. Maybe the yard boy—Brian? Bran? whatever his name is—maybe he really was so good at his frauds and hoaxes that he tricked his own family. So what? It's still criminal, what he did. And after what I've suffered already, I feel entirely justified insisting that they be prosecuted to the full extent of the law—"

Mrs. Marcus seemed to be arguing with Mrs. Stuldy, not me. But I interrupted.

"Won't you let me explain?" I asked.

And then I told them everything. I started off with Mom eloping with Dad and being disowned, and then never wanting to talk about her parents. Both Mrs. Marcus and Mrs. Stuldy listened intently. But by the time I got around to us moving into the Marcuses' house, Mrs. Marcus started interrupting with skeptical questions.

"You can't tell me your mother didn't recognize the name!" she said. "If your grandparents were Marcuses too."

"Bran, well, he tried to make it so she didn't suspect—he said stuff like you'd just lived in New York and Florida, not Ohio first. And he told her your name was pronounced a little differently— Mar-kees, not Marcus—and spelled differently, M-A-R-Q-U-I-S, and he hid everything that had your name spelled correctly. . . ."

"How stupid can your mother be?" Mrs. Marcus asked.

"Not stupid," I said. "Just . . . trusting. And—and I think she wanted to believe Bran. She wanted to believe this miraculous job had just fallen into his lap, had solved all our problems."

I told about how Mom wanted to be a doctor so badly, and how many obstacles she'd faced. And I told about myself too, how I'd found out Bran's secret but hadn't known what to do about it. I finished with Mrs. Marcus coming to the house that morning, and Mom being shocked and horrified and confused.

"I guess she was kind of rude to you," I said. "But that was just because she was so certain she was right and you were wrong. She'd never doubted Bran about anything before."

I fiddled with a teaspoon that was lying on the table in front of me. Nobody spoke. Then I looked directly at Mrs. Marcus.

"So, please, can you forgive us for what happened? I'm really sorry, and I know Mom and Bran are too. If you already called the police, can you tell them—"

"She didn't call the police," Mrs. Stuldy said.

Hearing that was like having a monster lifted off my back. I felt so light all of a sudden that I could have floated right up to the ceiling. But Mrs. Marcus was still frowning.

"*She* wouldn't let me," Mrs. Marcus said, inclining her head toward Mrs. Stuldy. "Said I needed a cooling-off period. She said there had to be more to the story than what I thought. And we could watch out the window and see you weren't carrying off any of my valuables. Or—not any that you hadn't already stolen."

"We haven't stolen anything!" I said heatedly. "Bran wouldn't even let us use your silverware!"

Mrs. Stuldy and Mrs. Marcus exchanged glances again.

"Oh, I don't know," Mrs. Marcus said. She looked more tired than ever. "My son didn't think I was even up to coming down here to put the house on the market. And now this . . . this girl acts like she really believes what she's saying, but what if she's just acting? Or what if her brother has really got her fooled? Why don't I just go ahead and call the police and let them sort everything out?"

Mrs. Stuldy cleared her throat.

"My son got picked up for shoplifting when he was thirteen," she said. "And we had all those 'get tough on crime' judges. They threw the book at him. His first offense. And after that it was like everyone thought of Sam as a criminal. So he became one. He was too weak to do anything different."

In my wildest dreams I couldn't imagine Bran turning into someone who robbed a bank and murdered someone and spent the rest of his life in prison. But I understood Mrs. Stuldy's point. It gave me chills.

Mrs. Marcus sighed.

"Go get your mother and brother," she said. "I want to talk to them."

What Mrs. Marcus did then was pretty smart, I thought. She made Mom and Bran tell the whole story over again, separately. She interviewed both of them in Mrs. Stuldy's kitchen, while the rest of us sat waiting on all the extra furniture in the living room.

Finally Mrs. Marcus walked heavily out of the kitchen, with a pale-faced Bran following her. Mrs. Marcus leaned against the back of one of the couches.

"Maybe you three are the best liars I've ever met. Or maybe you're a good family with a horrible history and one huge mistake." She narrowed her eyes a little, staring at Bran. His face turned red and he lowered his head in shame.

"I couldn't say for sure what you are," Mrs. Marcus continued. "But I know this is the biggest decision I've had to make since I started having to decide things on my own. I can ask myself what John would do, but I don't even know what that would be—this is too weird. But I guess—I guess if I'm going to make a mistake, I want it to be on the side of giving someone the benefit of the doubt. So as long as there's nothing missing from my house, I'm not going to call the police."

"Well, hot dang and good for you!" Mrs. Stuldy cheered, beaming. The rest of us were too numb to say a word.

But Mrs. Marcus wasn't done.

"I just want to say, I want all your things out of there today," she went on. "I want to sleep in my own house tonight."

Mom and Bran and I all looked at one another. We could hardly complain that Mrs. Marcus was being unfair, but where would we go? Even if we had the money for it, we couldn't move anywhere that quickly. And we didn't have any money. I remembered telling Bran we could always live in our car if we had to, but what would we do with our furniture?

Mom swallowed hard. I could tell she was thinking about dropping out of school and going back to work as a waitress, of being a waitress for the rest of her life.

"I understand," she said softly. I'd never felt so sorry for her in all my life. She looked like a whipped dog, too humiliated even to look Mrs. Marcus straight in the eye. "We—"

Mrs. Stuldy interrupted.

"You know, I've been thinking," she said, so casually you'd have thought we were just sitting around shooting the breeze, passing the time on a lazy summer day. "I've been thinking for the past week or so that I ought to rent me one of those storage units."

"Storage units?" I repeated. I thought Mrs. Stuldy had gone crazy with all the excitement.

"You know, one of those places you can store furniture you don't need right at the present time," Mrs. Stuldy said. "I doubt I have enough to fill a whole unit, so you'uns can put some of your things in with mine. That is, if you're not too proud to let your possessions go sharing space with a convict's."

We all stared at her like none of us understood English. Then as soon as I figured out what she was talking about, I said, "Oh, we're not. We're not too proud for that."

Mrs. Stuldy saved us, I thought. *If our furniture's in storage, we can live in the car after all.*

But she still had more to say.

"If I remember correctly after all this time, this house is right spacious when there's not a lot of extra furniture sitting around," she said. "Roy and me have two bedrooms we never use at all. Why don't the three of you just move on in with us?"

We lived at the Stuldys' for the rest of the summer. And it was such a relief—like walking into air-conditioning on a hot summer day, like sinking into a cozy bed when you're dead tired, like eating one of Mrs. Stuldy's cinnamon jumbles when you're starving.

That's what it felt like to live someplace people wanted us, after months of breathing stolen air.

Mom was all awkward and uncomfortable about it at first. She said it was only for one night, maybe two. Just until we found an apartment. Just until she found a job.

But then she and Mrs. Stuldy had a couple of late-night talks at the kitchen table. One night they were still there talking when I got up for breakfast. I don't know what all they said, but after that Mrs. Stuldy called Mom "child," just like she called me. And Mom didn't say anything else about moving out right away or dropping out of school.

Bran and Mom and I did all the work moving our furniture and Sam Stuldy's furniture into the storage unit. (Mrs. Stuldy was right: Her house did have a lot of space once all that furniture was gone.) Then Bran worked out a deal with Mrs. Marcus to make up for the cost of the utilities we'd used since May. He and I packed up all her things and loaded them onto a truck so a moving company could drive them back to New York for her.

Mrs. Marcus stood over us the whole time, watching us with narrowed eyes. She complained about fingerprints on the pictures, about tiny nicks in the paint on the living room walls—nicks that had probably been there long before Mom and Bran and I even saw the house. But she couldn't find anything missing.

"How can you stand her acting like that, all snotty and mean?" I asked Bran late one evening, after we'd worked for six hours straight and she hadn't even offered us a drink of water.

"It's what I deserve, Britt," Bran said. "I'm lucky it isn't worse."

And this was a totally new Bran, humbled and not nearly so sure of himself. I didn't know what to make of him.

I didn't know how to deal with Mrs. Marcus, either. I'd spent too much time staring at pictures, longing for her to love me. I had trouble even looking at her now, and I was glad when she finally flew back to New York, leaving behind a huge FOR SALE sign in the yard.

Bran cut her grass for free the rest of the summer. He mowed the Stuldys' grass too and worked with Mr. Stuldy around the house. They rewired the front porch lighting together; they fixed a leaky faucet in the bathroom; they painted the Stuldys' kitchen. When they opened the first can of paint, Mrs. Stuldy decided she had to start going to the senior center once again to get away from all the home improvement projects.

"It doesn't bother you anymore to go there?" I asked as I helped her pack up a box of applesauce cookies.

"Nope," she said. "Just because they talk, I don't have to listen." She grinned. "And if any of them start bragging about their grandchildren, I can always tell about how great you and Bran are."

I didn't feel like we were all that great anymore, but at least we hadn't murdered anyone. I glanced out toward the living room, which seemed almost empty without her son's furniture.

"Mrs. Stuldy," I said slowly, "it's not like you traded Sam for us, is it? You still love him, don't you?"

"Of course," she said. "I wouldn't be worth much if I couldn't love more than one person at a time, would I?"

"I guess not," I said.

She followed my gaze.

"Honey," she said. "That furniture wasn't doing Sam one bit of good sitting there. It was just making me sad. And now it's still waiting for him, and I'm still waiting for him, but I'm getting on with my life too. I didn't know how bad that furniture was making me feel until you told me."

"I did?" I said.

"Well, not in so many words. But every time you came in here, you looked at that living room like you felt sorry for me."

"Oh," I said.

I had other questions I wanted to ask her, but the senior center bus arrived for her then.

In August an official-looking letter arrived for Mom from Gulfstone University. Mrs. Stuldy kept it on the counter until Mom got home, and then we all clustered around her while she opened it. I felt like we were watching one of those awards shows, where a presenter pulls a slip of paper out of an envelope and announces, "And the Oscar goes to . . ."

Mom fumbled with the envelope and unfolded the letter

with trembling hands. I could see her eyes moving, reading it. But she didn't say anything.

"Well?" Bran prompted her. "Is it about the scholarship?"

"I—" Mom couldn't seem to go on. Her eyes filled with tears.

"Didn't you get it?" Bran asked in disbelief.

Mom shook her head. "I never had a chance," she whispered. "They've canceled the whole program."

We all stared at her in shock.

"Oh, child," Mrs. Stuldy murmured. "After all your hard work . . ."

Mom brushed away her tears. "I never should have gotten my hopes up," she said. "I knew they were making budget cuts. I was just fool enough to think I had another year. I thought this summer had bought me enough time to get through before they shut it all down." She grimaced. It hurt to watch the pain sweep over her face.

"This is like a sign, isn't it?" She choked out. "A sign that maybe I'm not supposed to be a doctor. Maybe I'm not even supposed to be a college graduate." She crumpled the letter and let it fall to the floor. "Everything about this summer was wrong. Even if I'd gotten the scholarship, it would have been tainted—tainted by Bran's lies and us living in the Marcuses' house illegally—I'm sorry, Bran, but it's true. Even if I'd gotten the scholarship, it probably would have been wrong to take it."

Bran looked like Mom had slapped him. Hearing Mom talk like that was probably worse punishment than every single one of Mrs. Marcus's nasty looks and heavy boxes.

I wanted to tell Mom that plenty of good things had happened this summer. Yes, Bran had lied, but I'd met Mrs. Stuldy, too. Yes, we'd made a big mistake moving into the Marcuses' house, but Mrs. Marcus had forgiven us. That ought to count for something. The Stuldys letting us move in with them ought to count for something too.

I couldn't bring myself to say any of that to Mom when she looked so wild and disappointed. I bent down and picked up the Gulfstone University letter.

"Now, Becky, child," Mrs. Stuldy said. "You shouldn't talk like that. If nobody ever built anything good on top of bad, the world would be a really sorry place. That letter's not a sign that you should quit. It's just another obstacle you've got to climb past."

I smoothed out the letter and looked at it. It started out, *We regret to inform you . . .* But I kept reading. The very last paragraph began, *However, due to your superior academic achievement, we can offer you . . .*

"Mom!" I shrieked. "Mom! Did you read the whole letter? They can't give you the single-mothers scholarship, but you qualify for a different one just because you're smart! It's— look!"

"What?" Mom said. She took the letter I held out to her. But she didn't start screaming and cheering. She just stood there in a daze.

What if she thought this scholarship was tainted too? What if she turned it down?

"Mom," I said. "You've got to take this scholarship. You didn't get it because of Bran lying. You got it because you worked hard and Bran believed in you and the Stuldys helped us and Mrs. Marcus forgave us. And you have to forgive Bran too for what he did. Don't be like your parents. Be like Mrs. Stuldy, who bakes cookies for the women who talk mean about her. Look what she built on top of her son's crime. She could have said we were criminals too and she wanted nothing to do with us. But she didn't. She took us in." The words came out so fast I felt like they were tripping off my tongue. Everyone was staring at me. But I didn't need to look to Bran or Mrs. Stuldy or anyone else to make sure I was saying the right thing.

I kept talking.

"It's like—remember how you said pigs and goats and humans all look the same when they're embryos? Well, you're sort of the embryo version of a doctor. And you can go ahead and become one or you can give up. And that's what would be wrong. Giving up."

I wasn't sure Mom understood what I meant. But then she smiled and drew me into a hug.

"Of course I'll accept this scholarship," she said over the top of my head. "But thank you, Britt. Thank you for making everything so clear."

Mom reached out and hugged Bran, too, and it was like she was forgiving him, right then.

"I think this calls for a celebration," Mrs. Stuldy said, beaming. "How about some chocolate cake?"

At the end of August we left the Stuldys to move into an apartment at the university. But we go back and visit a lot. I tell Mrs. Stuldy about the friends I'm making at school; she tells me about the friends she's making at the senior center. And Bran helps Mr. Stuldy.

Sometimes when I'm over at the Stuldys' I can't help staring at the Marcuses' house. No one new has moved in yet, and it looks empty and sad. No matter how much I squint, I can't make it look as glorious to me as it did at the beginning of the summer. I see the cracks in the stucco now; I can tell the bushes need to be trimmed and the shed needs a fresh coat of paint.

It's hard to look at that house without feeling ashamed.

But I don't blame Bran anymore. The other day I found him picking up palm fronds that had blown down in the Marcuses' yard.

"Did Mrs. Marcus tell you to do that?" I asked.

"No," he said.

"She already forgave you," I said. "She isn't ever going to *like* you."

"I know," Bran said. "But this helps me forgive myself."

And I knew just what he meant. I know now that Bran isn't perfect. But somehow that makes me love him even more.

When Mom goes to the Stuldys' with us, sometimes she talks about her parents. I think Mrs. Stuldy told her that I needed to hear more about them, and Mom feels safe talking there. So now I know what Mom's life was like when she was my age: how her parents would lock her in her room for an entire day for not finishing her oatmeal at breakfast, how they'd spank her until she bruised just because she spilled her milk. And now I know about the two brothers who died when she was little, and how Mom thinks maybe that's what turned her parents so sour.

All her stories are sad, and I can understand why she didn't want to talk before. But I still wonder: What if her parents have changed? What if now that they're old they regret being so mean and driving her away?

Last night, with Mom's permission, I wrote to my grandparents. I picked out a pretty postcard—you can't send that back unopened—and I printed carefully on the back:

Dear Mr. and Mrs. Marcus,

You don't know me, but I'm your granddaughter. A few months ago, someone I thought might be my grandfather died. And I was really sad. It didn't seem fair that he had died without me knowing anything about him. So I was just wondering what you were like. Do you have any hobbies? What do you do for fun? What makes you happy?

If you don't want to know me, that's okay. But shouldn't I get a chance to know you?

Sincerely,

Britt Lassiter

P.S. You should be really proud of your daughter now.

Just for good measure, I wrote a postcard almost like it to my other grandparents. I wrote my dad, too. I mailed all three cards after school, on my way to visit Mrs. Stuldy.

Mom says I shouldn't get my hopes up, and probably none of my relatives will answer me. And even if they do, I may not like what I find out. I told her that's okay. I just had to try.

Probably someday when I have kids of my own, I'll want to tell them the story of this summer. I know just how I'll start. I'll say, *Your uncle Bran was up to something.* And I'll tell them what a great detective I was, and how scared and confused I was when I found out the truth. I'll tell them about Mrs. Stuldy, too, and how much she helped. And I'll be able to finish the story, *In spite of all the mistakes Bran and I made, everything turned out better in the end.*